DEAD MAN'S FLOAT

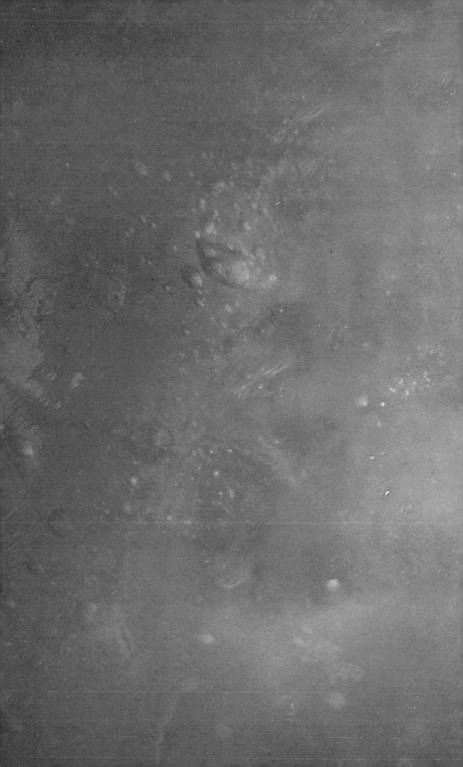

DEAD MAN'S FLOAT

SHAWN SARLES

SCHOLASTIC INC.

The publisher does not have any control over and does not assume any responsibility for author or third-party websites or their content.

This book is a work of fiction. Names, characters, places, and incidents are either the product of the author's imagination or are used fictitiously, and any resemblance to actual persons, living or dead, business establishments, events, or locales is entirely coincidental.

ISBN 978-1-339-00283-5

10 9 8 7 6 5 4 3 2 1   23 24 25 26 27

Printed in the U.S.A.   40

First printing, September 2023

Book design by Christopher Stengel

For Kyle

CHAPTER
ONE

Sam stood at the end of the world, knees knocking, her breath coming in short bursts. Even with her eyes squeezed shut, she could sense the cold emptiness stretching out before her. A void just beyond her reach. She dared a peek through the slits of her eyelids and almost lost her balance. The height was dizzying, the water frighteningly far away. It was still and dark beneath her, a mirror reflecting her impossibly tiny self.

"Are you gonna jump?" a voice called up from below, echoing off the rafters. "Or are you too scared?"

Sam gulped as an unlikely wind brushed across her bare shoulders, causing a fresh wave of goose bumps to sizzle and pop along her neck. The taunt confirmed that she didn't have a choice. She was a prisoner condemned to walk the plank. She had nowhere to go but forward. And down.

Her toes curled over the edge of the platform as she took

another look at the pool below. Ten meters wasn't so bad. Only a few stories. She'd seen divers throw themselves from this height, twisting and flipping, contorting their bodies into painful pretzels and then breaking through the surface headfirst. If they could survive all that, then surely, she could survive one jump.

"We're waiting," the voice rang out again. But this time it was followed by a stage whisper loud enough for even Sam to hear. "Told you she'd chicken out."

A few laughs rose from the pool deck, and Sam knew she couldn't stall any longer.

Sucking in a deep breath, she inhaled the moisture and chlorine in the air, the familiar scent burning her lungs and steadying her nerves. She closed her eyes again and listened for the water as it beckoned to her, lapping lightly, trickling and moving in nearly imperceptible currents. She listened until her legs stopped shaking. Until a calmness washed over her.

Then she reached up, plugged her nose, and took that final step off the ledge, solid ground disappearing underneath her in a heart-stopping second.

Falling was the terrifying part. Wind rushed through her hair, yanking it to the sky, letting her know that she'd made a grave mistake as it tried to pull her back onto the platform. Her stomach flipped and her mouth puckered into a grimace. But she didn't scream. She didn't make a sound as she plummeted. As a memory flashed in her head.

Her six-year-old self. A leap from a pier on a summer day. Laughter bubbling up in the muggy afternoon. A plunge into murky lake water, cold and consuming.

She sank into that chilly darkness, the water covering her shoulders and then her head. She opened her eyes and saw another pair of legs next to hers. She spotted another arm sculling through the water. Long strands of brown hair rippled in the depths and Sam dove down, following her best friend, Kasey, as if they were mermaids.

The water grew colder as they swam deeper, the summer sun not strong enough to penetrate all the way down to the bottom of the lake, where long, ropy reeds sprang up in bunches, blocking their way. But they just pushed them aside, using their hands to part the vegetation like curtains. The grassy stalks tickled Sam's arms as she moved past them, as she searched for sunken treasure. Goose bumps exploded up the back of her neck, a thrilling chill even as her lungs tightened, as she realized she was almost out of breath. She reached forward and tapped Kasey's foot, pointing up toward the surface. Her cheeks bulged as a mouthful of air escaped her lips. Kasey nodded in understanding, and they both turned, the reeds swirling around their kicking feet, getting one last touch in before Sam and Kasey rocketed to the surface.

But as they pushed off the muddy bottom of the lake, the reeds didn't fall away. They wrapped their slimy tendrils around their ankles and held tight, trapping them under the surface as the seconds ticked by, as their lungs contracted, as panic rose in their chests and they tried desperately to pull themselves free.

Sam looked over at Kasey, her eyes wide and scared, her lungs on fire. But she didn't know what to do. The harder she kicked, the more tightly the reeds wound around her ankle, creating an ironclad hold that anchored her in the deep. That kept her from a lifesaving breath.

A sharp ringing had pierced her ears as the pressure in her chest built, as her vision grew blurry, as realization stole over her, despair. She lifted her head and screamed, losing the rest of her air, the gas escaping in a violent jellyfish bloom that rushed to the surface, her last breath abandoning her.

And then she started to slip deeper, the water turning icy cold even as her chest burned with an excruciating pain. She kept sinking, the reeds pulling her under, until the darkness enveloped her completely. Until, suddenly, she couldn't feel anything anymore.

She could still conjure up that strange sensation, that new numbness. Like she'd been transported to a different dimension. She had been all alone, floating in a vast emptiness. Even Kasey had disappeared from her side. It was a horrifying place devoid of sights and sounds and all feeling, where she seemed to float on and on in an utterly black ocean, the fathomless nothingness more frightening than the pain she'd been in before.

Oblivion.

Sam crashed through the pool's surface, the drop from the ten-meter platform over in only a couple of seconds. The impact stung the soles of her feet and jarred her back to the present. But as she let herself sink deeper under the water, she recalled how, just when she'd given up, her father's arm had appeared out of nowhere and dug her from that lake grave. His strength had been enough to snap the reeds' hold, to pull her to the surface and onto the dock, where she'd taken heaving breaths until she'd thrown up, her vomit green and chunky like she'd exorcised a demon.

But he hadn't been able to get to Kasey in time.

While Sam was still throwing up on the dock, her best friend's body had bobbed to the surface and floated there, facedown, lifeless. The empty shell of a girl. And even though Sam knew that there was nothing she could have done to save Kasey, that she'd barely made it out of that accident alive, she still blamed herself. She was only six years old then, but she should have been stronger. She should have been able to rip Kasey from the reeds' grasp. She should have swum them both to the surface. To fresh air. To safety.

Sam's toes grazed the bottom of the pool and she let herself settle. She exhaled a stream of air and sank deeper, tilting her head back and squinting to look up. The ten-meter platform seemed even farther away from down here, but it didn't frighten her anymore. She felt calm and at peace. Powerful, even.

The water didn't scare her like it had when she was six.

She'd mastered that fear. Made it her dominion. She might have failed Kasey, but now, nine years later, she wouldn't let that happen again. She wouldn't let anyone else drown on her watch.

The shadows of her new teammates swayed above her, their bodies gathered around the edge of the pool, peering down at her, most likely looking for any sign of weakness. But Sam didn't care what those girls thought about her. She wasn't a coward and she'd proven that. Practice would start tomorrow, and she'd show them what she could really do. How fast she could go. No one would care about how long it'd taken her to jump off the high dive then. No one would whisper that she was chicken.

Feeling her lungs starting to cave, Sam blew out another stream of bubbles. Then she raised her arms and pressed them into a straight arrow. She bent her knees and pushed off the bottom of the pool, dolphin kicking to propel herself faster through the water until she broke the surface, sending up a spray in every direction. She breathed in and out as she treaded water, looking until she spotted the owner of the voice that had taunted her earlier—the girls' team captain: Bailey Miller.

"What a rush," Sam chirped, laying it on thick as she watched the girl squirm.

Bailey stood there with her arms crossed and a scowl contorting her lips into something unpleasant. She was clearly upset, and Sam had to dip her chin lower in the water to make sure she hid her grin. Because if Bailey was mad now, she'd only feel worse after practice tomorrow.

"We've all done it," Bailey scoffed, uncrossing her arms and picking at her fingernails. "Now hurry up and dry off. We've gotta get out of here before someone catches us. We aren't supposed to be in here."

And they weren't. But somehow Bailey had a key to the pool—probably something the outgoing team captain had passed on to her—which they'd used to break in after school. Every new swimmer had been told to strip down to their suits and jump from the ten-meter platform, a plunge in the dark that had taken some people longer than others, and that a couple of people hadn't attempted at all.

"Let's go." Bailey clapped her hands together, everyone jumping into action as the crack echoed off the pool walls. She took one last disapproving look at Sam and then turned, making her way to the door without a glance back.

Sam watched as everyone started moving, and then she waded to the wall and pulled herself up in one motion. She grabbed her nearby towel and wrapped it around her shoulders, using it to dry off her hair, which she kept short so it'd fit under a cap more easily. No one seemed to notice her as they filed out, which was fine. She didn't need to be the center of attention. She preferred to be left alone. She had one goal and didn't like distractions.

She peered back at the pool, the waves she'd made smoothed

over already so that the surface looked clean and clear and crystalline. Her fingers itched to slice through the water. Every pool was different. They had their own personalities. And she wondered what this one might hold.

Something dripped into the water, and Sam looked down, puzzling over the swirl of color there, the red fading to pink before it eventually dissipated. Another drop fell, this one crimson and impossible to mistake.

Sam's hand flew to her face, and her fingers slid over the warm slick of blood dribbling over her lips and down her chin. Panic thundered in her ears, and she leaned her head forward, sniffling as she pressed her towel to her nose. A metallic tang still managed to seep down her throat and she gagged, choking on the bitter taste. Her eyes darted from side to side, but no one seemed to have noticed. Most everyone had already trickled out. Which was good. She could deal with this. She'd been getting nosebleeds for what felt like her entire life. She had a supply of cotton balls in her bag. She just needed to wash off real quick.

Sam startled as she caught sight of a reflection in the pool. It wavered in front of her, mirroring her shadow. But it wasn't her. Its hair was too long. Its eyes red embers that glowed like drops of blood in the water.

Kasey, Sam thought, fear prickling the hairs on her scalp as her hand reached up to clasp the thin necklace pressed against the wet skin of her collarbone.

But then she remembered herself. Remembered that Kasey was dead. That her guilt was playing tricks on her.

With a quick motion, Sam dipped her hand in the pool and dispelled the reflection. She cupped a handful of water and splashed it against her face. She used her towel to pat her cheeks dry, and then jumped to her feet, her head tilted down, sucking in breaths through her mouth to keep the blood at bay. She waddled over to her bag and dug through it until she found the cotton balls, pushing one into her nostril and feeling almost immediate relief. Crisis averted.

Wiping her nose and chin again, Sam turned back to the pool. It'd look different tomorrow morning, with all the lane lines put in and the backstroke flags flapping. But it'd be home. Or, at least, a home away from home. Her new training ground.

She gave herself a final pat down, then pulled on her sweatpants and a hoodie. She draped her towel over her wet hair, doing her best to hide the cotton ball stuck up her nose. She'd take it out when she got home. But right now she couldn't afford to show any weakness. She wanted to get off on the right foot with these girls. She wanted them to know that she meant business. She didn't play around in the pool. Hopefully, they'd respect that. Because she needed them to push her. She needed their help to make herself faster. And if they weren't serious, then they better stay out of her way.

CHAPTER
TWO

The water churned in front of Sam's face as Bailey's feet kicked up a splash that made it difficult to see. Sam didn't drop back, though. She kept right on Bailey's tail, inching closer with each stroke, itching to pull ahead. That morning, when Coach Hendricks had assigned them to the same lane, Sam had let Bailey lead—not that Bailey had given her much choice. But the warm-up was over. They were into the main set now. And Bailey, even though she was good, was going too slow.

With a burst of speed, Sam closed the gap, reached out, and tapped Bailey's foot. It was swimming etiquette. A signal to let Bailey know that Sam wanted to pass. At the next wall, the girl would pause and let Sam go by. It was courtesy. The lanes were narrow, only wide enough for one person to go up while another came down. Which was why they swam in a circle, a chain of girls moving counterclockwise through the pool.

Sam focused back in, realizing that she'd let her mind slip. She needed to stay present and intentional. Every stroke mattered. Every lap and every set. Every second Sam didn't push herself was a second lost. If she wasn't practicing at her best, she wouldn't compete at her best. She wouldn't get faster. Which was what she needed. The whole reason they'd moved here in the first place.

Coming to the end of the lane, Sam kicked harder, readying to accelerate through the turn, past Bailey, and into the lead. Only, when Bailey got to the wall, she didn't pull up. She didn't let Sam pass. She just flipped and pushed straight off, dolphin kicking a few times before popping up and continuing on her way. Sam was so shocked that she almost missed her own turn. But she managed to save it, catching up with a few well-timed strokes, falling back into Bailey's wake.

Sam tried not to jump to conclusions. Maybe Bailey hadn't felt her tap. Maybe it'd been too gentle. Sam just needed to make it more obvious. With another burst of speed, she pulled close and tapped Bailey's foot again, sliding her fingers from the girl's heel to her toes to make her presence known. Then, for good measure, she did it again.

This time, Bailey's foot tapped back, fluttering frantically and knocking Sam's hand out of the way. As they approached the next turn, Sam got ready to move ahead, but Bailey kept going, ignoring her again.

What was happening?

Sam's ears burned as she turned, slingshotting off the wall in pursuit of her captain. Bailey had definitely felt her that time. Which meant that she didn't care. Or was just plain rude. Either way, Sam wasn't going to let her get away with it. She wouldn't jeopardize her training to stroke Bailey's ego.

Accelerating, it took everything in Sam not to yank Bailey back by the ankle. Instead, she tapped the girl's foot. Once. Twice. Three times. And then a fourth for good measure. She stuck close, the waves from Bailey's kick hitting her squarely in the jaw. She couldn't really breathe in the midst of all that white water, but she didn't need to. Not until she got ahead.

Coming to the wall again, Bailey flipped, her eyes meeting Sam's through their goggles for a split second, her teeth gritted in a sneer as she kept going. Sam didn't miss a beat this time, though. She turned right after Bailey, pushing off hard as she made her decision. If Bailey wouldn't let her pass, then Sam would just have to swim around her.

Checking that it was clear, Sam edged into the middle of the lane. She stuck close to Bailey, swimming right beside her. She put her head down and dug in, gaining an inch with each pull. Next to her, she could feel Bailey shifting gears, picking up her turnover rate as she stroked harder.

When they got to the wall, they were dead even. But neither pulled up. They turned together and pushed off, both gliding underwater, letting momentum carry them farther and faster. They broke the surface at the same time and charged down the pool, sprinting as they tried to beat the other. They crowded into the same half of the lane, their fingers brushing on their recoveries, their heads turning to breathe at the same time. But it didn't slow either of them down.

Sam was surprised that Bailey could stay with her. Most girls with that kind of bark didn't have the bite to back it up. But as they bore down on the final twenty-five yards of the set, Sam kicked it up a notch. She dug deeper and cut through the water, her lungs burning in her chest as she pulled ahead by a hand and then an elbow. When the wall came into sight, she poured it on and lunged forward, timing it perfectly, touching first.

Bailey came in a half second later. And when she touched the wall, she immediately stood up and ripped off her goggles to glare at Sam.

"Who the hell do you think you are?" she wheezed, barely able to get the question out between huffed breaths.

"Samantha Marquess. State champion."

There was a satisfaction in saying it, even though Sam didn't like coming off as an egotistical brat. But the facts were the facts. She had won two races at the state championships last winter. The freshman phenom.

"I've never heard of you," Bailey sputtered.

"Different state," Sam explained, shrugging. "You can look it up if you don't believe me."

Bailey's mouth gaped open, and Sam could practically see

all the catty thoughts running through the girl's head. It didn't bother her, though. She'd dealt with this kind of jealousy before. Everyone wanted to be the best. Not even Sam was immune to that. She just took it more seriously. It was how she stood out. The way she could earn a scholarship to a top school and maybe even make the Olympic team. It was how she proved that she was the best.

"That's what I like to see."

Bailey's mouth snapped shut as Coach Hendricks came over, clapping his clipboard while he studied his stopwatch. The rest of the girls were finishing up the set, coming into the wall and craning their heads over to see what all the commotion was about. Most of them looked nervous. Worried about what their captain might do. They seemed unsure of Sam and how her arrival might upset the order of things. How it might topple their leader from the top spot. But a couple of girls, Sam noticed even though they did their best to hide their small smiles under the waves, seemed pleased to find Bailey in such a huff. The majority was definitely stacked against her, but Sam had at least a few allies among the team's ranks.

"Impressive stuff," Coach Hendricks went on. "Especially for the first practice of the year."

The girls nodded as they turned toward him. But Sam could still feel their attention drifting to her. Could sense the gossip they were desperate to share with each other. Sam tried to shake it off, though. She tried to keep focused on her new coach. She'd only met him once, but she'd overheard her dad talking to him on the phone plenty of times. He had an enthusiastic coaching style. He was a positive motivator. Which must have worked, since he had several regional and state championships to his name. He had a proven track record. It was the reason why Sam's dad had brought her here out of all the high school programs in the area.

"I want to see more of that," Coach Hendricks went on. "Sam, why don't you take the lead on this next set. And, Bailey, keep up the hard work. If you stick with her, you're gonna have a great senior season. A little friendly rivalry never hurt anyone."

But as Sam took in Bailey's sour expression, she wasn't so sure about that. It looked like Bailey would gladly drown her if given the chance. If that was what it took to remain on top.

Good thing Sam didn't plan on getting caught.

CHAPTER
THREE

"So they, like, recruited you?" In the locker room, Sam turned to find a short girl she hadn't met yet staring up at her. "Doesn't seem very fair to the rest of us."

"I—I wasn't recruited," Sam stuttered, thrown by the accusation.

And she hadn't been. Not by Coach Hendricks, at least. It was more her dad who had done the recruiting, researching high school programs and reaching out to them. He'd set up interviews and tours. He'd put together a whole spreadsheet with pros and cons, measuring each program by its training facilities, its coaching staff, its results. He hadn't felt Sam was being pushed enough at her old school. He thought she wasn't getting the attention she deserved. He thought she wouldn't be ready for the next level if they didn't make a move.

"Well . . ." The girl held the syllable on her tongue, the

word buzzing against her tongue like an alarm bell. "That's what Bailey said."

"You know, you really should mind your own business."

Sam turned as a new girl came up behind them and saved her from the awkward exchange with a flick of her hand and a shooing motion that worked perfectly in getting this small interloper to move along.

"You have to ignore Paige," the girl said, turning to face Sam once they were alone. "She's got her head shoved so far up Bailey's butt. Like just about everyone else on the team."

"But not you?"

The girl paused as if she had to mull it over. "No. Not me."

Sam recognized her now as one of the girls who had found pleasure in Bailey's tantrum, and she relaxed, relieved that she could let her guard down for a second.

"She's dating my brother," the girl explained. "Clark. So I'm resistant to her charms. I don't know what he sees in her. She's kind of a monster."

Sam laughed, delighted by this girl's unflinching honesty. She was also happy to have someone on her side. Someone who she could be anti-Bailey with.

"I'm Caroline, by the way."

"Sam."

The girls shook hands, a gesture that seemed too formal for teammates. But Sam didn't know what else to do.

"We were in the same lane this morning?" Sam asked,

vaguely remembering Caroline's face now. Everyone looked so different when their hair and features weren't obscured by a cap and goggles. Caroline's was long and curly and so dark it almost appeared black. Sam imagined it would look like a squid-ink cloud underwater. An aura to hide in. Or to sneak attack from.

"Yeah, that was me bringing up the rear. I think you might have even lapped me once. Or twice."

"You'll get there." It was Sam's turn to be nice. "It's only the first day."

Caroline nodded, as if Sam's belief was all she needed. And then the conversation kind of faltered between them. Sam wasn't good at this. At making friends. It was why she hadn't fought her dad on transferring to a new school. She hadn't had any real relationships back home. Teammates, sure. But most of them resented her. Or just ignored her, thinking she was a freak for being so focused. For having her whole life revolve around swimming. Friendship had never seemed necessary to achieving her goals. And it guaranteed she wouldn't get hurt again. That she wouldn't lose anyone else.

Sam's hand snaked up to her neck, searching for her necklace. She jolted, spinning around and scrambling to get back into her locker, frantically turning the dial, messing up the combination in her panic. But then she had her locker open. She had her water bottle in hand. And her necklace was right there where she'd left it during practice, the golden seashell charm glinting in the light, as small and delicate as a fish scale. She unlooped it from around the bottle and clasped it behind her neck. She pressed it to her chest and felt calm again. Felt Kasey's presence looking over her.

A hair dryer snapped on, and Sam came back to herself. She turned and saw Caroline staring at her, no doubt regretting her decision to befriend the new, weird girl.

"Do you need to get in there?" Caroline asked, pointing to the row of girls getting ready, primping and spritzing and applying lip gloss. "I can throw a few elbows if you need some mirror space."

This surprised Sam. And made her feel bad that she'd jumped to conclusions about Caroline.

"No. I'm good. My hair dries super fast." Sam pointed to her page cut and tried her best to appear nonchalant. To seem cool.

"That's smart." Caroline nodded again. "And short hair looks so good on you. I wish I could pull it off. But I just end up looking like my brother. Like, disturbingly so."

Sam caught herself laughing again. And she liked it.

"Wanna grab breakfast?" Caroline asked without skipping a beat. "I'm starving."

"Oh, they provide that for us?"

She had packed a protein bar, a yogurt, and two bananas just to be safe.

"Yeah," Caroline explained as she led Sam out of the locker

room. "The parents bring it in. Depending on whose turn it is, it can be anything from plain bagels to homemade biscuits. Fingers crossed it's something good for our first day back."

Caroline pumped her fist as they entered the office connected to the pool and she spotted the morning's haul.

"Ham and cheese croissants," she cheered, and she immediately dug in.

Sam held back for a second, taking in the yeasty smell of warm bread and the salty tang of the ham. Her stomach growled, and she realized how hungry she was. How hard she must have worked during practice. She waded in next to Caroline and grabbed her own sandwich, nibbling at it more daintily than her new friend, who was already tearing through seconds.

The rest of the team was spread out around the room, talking with their mouths full, stopping only to take swigs of orange juice. It was mostly the boys, their hair still damp, falling in disheveled mops across their foreheads. Sam hadn't been able to take much stock of them during practice since Coach Hendricks had split them into their own lanes, even though Sam could have kept up.

"Clark, this is Sam, the new girl who beat your girlfriend today." Caroline cackled as she brought Sam over to a table and introduced her older brother. He only grunted back at them, though, turning to continue his conversation with the boys.

It didn't take much effort to see the resemblance between

the two. They had shockingly similar features for non-twins. Caroline was a sophomore like Sam, while Clark was a senior, the same year as Bailey, her boys' team captain counterpart. Sam recognized his crew cut and broad shoulders from the fast boys' lane where he'd taken the lead all morning, the alpha dog.

"Ignore him," Caroline said, not at all affected by his cold shoulder. "He's rude."

Then she took Sam's arm and led her over to an open table.

"Are there any plain croissants left?" a different boy asked as he fell into the chair next to Caroline.

"Relax," she replied. "I saved you one, since you're always the last boy out of the locker room."

"It takes time to look this good," the boy scoffed, gesturing to his extremely put-together self. "I've got to dry my hair and put product in it. You don't expect me to walk around all day with split ends and a cowlick, do you?"

Caroline rolled her eyes, but she still slid a package wrapped in tinfoil and marked with a V over to him. Which made Sam wonder. Were they dating?

"You know you're not the only vegetarian on the team," Caroline said.

"Yeah. But I'm the cutest one."

"Debatable."

The boy clutched at his heart, acting like Caroline had wounded him. And in that overdramatic performance, Sam knew that they weren't boyfriend and girlfriend. Maybe just best friends.

"Who's this?" the boy asked as he recovered and tore open the croissant, double-checking that it was meat-free before he started taking small bites.

"Duncan, meet Sam. Bailey's new nemesis."

A spark flickered in Duncan's eyes as he set his sandwich aside.

"Nemesis? I like the sound of that."

"I don't think I'd go that far," Sam mumbled, blushing at the attention. It'd been forever since she'd had a friend. And now she was maybe making two in one day.

"Don't listen to her," Caroline cut in. "They're totally rivals. You should have seen Bailey's face when Coach Hendricks told Sam to take the lead. There was literally steam coming out of her ears."

"But that was just the pool," Sam jumped in, trying to speak practically. "There was steam coming off all of us. It has to do with body temperature and the moisture in the air—"

But Sam didn't get a chance to finish as the door to the room flew open to reveal Bailey standing there, her hair dry and immaculately straightened, her pursed mouth covered in red lipstick as if she were out for blood. Sam's blood, in particular.

Her hands sat on her hips and her eyes swept across the room, coming to an abrupt halt when they landed on Sam.

Their eyes met, electricity flying between them. Then Bailey stomped into the room and came right up to her, as if that was somehow intimidating.

"Tonight," Bailey huffed. "Mandatory team meeting. I expect everyone to be there. Especially you. No excuses."

Sam could feel everyone in the room watching her. Waiting for her to crumble. But she stood her ground, keeping her shoulders back and her head high. People liked to under-estimate her. And she liked proving them wrong.

"See you tonight," Sam replied, her voice unwavering. She'd already jumped off the ten-meter platform in the dark. She didn't think Bailey could throw anything worse at her.

"Hope you don't scare easy," Bailey hissed. Then she turned and strode out of the room, leaving without even grabbing breakfast.

"Yeah." Duncan leaned in and whispered, filling the void left by Bailey's spite. "She's totally got it out for you. Nemeses times a thousand. This should be fun."

Only, Sam wasn't so sure about that.

CHAPTER
FOUR

The sun had started to set as Sam and Caroline got out of Duncan's car. Sam was still processing the fact that they'd invited her to join them, that she actually might have found friends. Duncan volunteered to drive, which had been a lifesaver since Sam wasn't sure she could have convinced her dad to let her come out if he knew where they were going. Luckily, a vague mention of team bonding had been enough to sway him. Not that she would have been able to tell him. She didn't know where they were or what they were going to do if he had asked for more details. Bailey had texted out the location during lunch. But even with the three of them putting their heads together, they couldn't figure out what she had planned. Sam had just assured her dad that she wouldn't stay late. That she'd be home early enough to keep on her sleep schedule. To get the maximum amount of rest needed for her body to recover before the next morning's practice.

"Well, this feels sufficiently creepy," Duncan said, taking a quick look around as he double-checked that he'd locked the car. "Are you sure she's not setting us up?"

"That's her ride over there," Caroline pointed out. "Right next to my brother's."

It was a coed kind of team meeting, unlike the previous night, when it'd only been the girls who'd snuck into the school to jump off the high dive.

"I forgot this park existed," Caroline went on, frowning as she took it all in. "When's the last time you were out here?"

"Not since I was a kid," Duncan replied. "I thought they'd torn it down."

Which they probably should have. It seemed pretty much abandoned. Tall grass and weeds stuck up through gaping cracks in the parking lot asphalt. There were broken benches and overflowing trash cans lining the area, and a sign stood near the entrance that Sam had to squint at to make out because the letters had faded so badly.

WENTWORTH PUBLIC PARK.

She felt sorry for the place. And wondered what had happened to it. How had it fallen into such disrepair?

Sam jumped as something shrieked behind her. She spun around and spotted the nearby playground. Another groan rose into the air as the swing set began to move, the rusted chains whining as if a child had begun to swing their legs even though the seat was empty. Probably just the wind.

"I think we're supposed to be over there," Caroline said, tilting her chin toward a fenced-in area on the other side of the parking lot. And they all turned and watched as shadows began to disappear through the chain link.

"You ready?" Duncan asked, and Sam knew the question was meant for her.

"Let's go," she said, clamping down on her nerves, not exactly sure she was telling the truth but thankful that she didn't have to go in there alone.

Sam had spent the last month and a half of school on her own. An extreme introvert. Going to class and turning in her homework assignments. Throwing in a pool session with her dad at the YMCA every day after school. She hadn't realized how lonely she'd been until this morning, when she'd met Caroline and Duncan. But they seemed to welcome her instantly. Seemed to have her back. Which left her wondering why she'd kept to herself for so long. What had she been so afraid of?

Her fingers drifted up to her chest and found the imprint of Kasey's necklace under her shirt, the seashell charm sitting right over her heart as she realized she already knew the answer to her own question. She patted it and took a deep breath. Then she plunged forward after Caroline and Duncan, trying not to lose pace with her two new friends.

The grass tugged at their feet as they left the parking lot

and trudged across the adjacent field. When they got closer to the fenced-in area, they started to hear murmurs, the rumbling of people who were too nervous or scared or uncomfortable to speak in normal voices.

"You made it," Bailey cackled, pushing off the fence where she'd been hiding in the shadows. "I thought for sure you'd bail."

"And miss the chance to see your ghoulish face?" Caroline exclaimed, clapping her hands together in mock delight.

Bailey's smile didn't falter, though. Those same bright red lips from the morning only perked up, the corners of her mouth turning into something wicked.

"After you," Bailey said. She swept her arms wide and moved to the side, revealing a hole that someone had made in the chain link. Sam hoped Bailey hadn't done it herself, that she didn't have a pair of wire cutters tucked into her back pocket. Was she about to frame Sam for vandalism? On top of trespassing? Get her arrested and kicked off the team? Was that her master plan?

Knowing there was nothing else she could do, Sam sighed and ducked her head. She squeezed through to the other side, Caroline and Duncan coming in right behind her.

"Oh, wow," Caroline whispered, taking in their surroundings. "I forgot there was a pool here."

"An empty pool," Duncan clarified, scrunching his nose up as if he'd smelled a skunk. "Or more like a giant hole in the ground."

And that was exactly what it was. A gaping, dried-up void in the earth. Sam had never seen anything like it. Twenty-five yards long and six lanes wide, a regulation-size pool without any water. It seemed wrong. And dangerous. They'd at least taken out the diving board, but that wouldn't exactly prevent someone from stumbling into the pool and cracking their head open. Shouldn't they have filled it in with cement? Or covered it with one of those tarps?

"You all going to join us?"

Sam's whole body tensed as Bailey slinked up behind them again. For a split second, she thought the girl meant to shove her into the pool. But instead, she pointed a manicured finger down into the deep end, and Sam had to blink as she noticed the rest of the team assembled there. She didn't know how she'd missed them before. They were all kind of milling around, squatting and leaning against the pool walls. Some of them looked nervous, while others appeared bored, scrolling through their phones, waiting for whatever Bailey had planned to start.

"We don't have all night," Bailey said, turning away. She walked toward the shallow end and carefully lowered herself into the pool.

Sam followed, opting to use one of the metal ladders instead of going right over the edge. She didn't want to hurt herself, and she wasn't exactly in a hurry to get down there.

"Have you all done this before?" Sam whispered, turning

back to Caroline and Duncan as she mounted the rickety ladder.

"Never," Duncan replied.

"The high dive is something we do every year with the new swimmers," Caroline added. "I had to do it last year as a freshman. But this? I have no idea what Bailey's thinking."

Sam nodded. Apparently tonight was going to be a surprise for everyone.

Her feet crunched on gravel and broken tile as she stepped down into the pool. Probably some shards of glass, too. She released her hold on the ladder and backed away to give Duncan and Caroline space. The pool's plastic lining wobbled underneath her. It cracked and moved, cleaving apart in places like a frozen-over lake. There was ground right beneath it, so Sam had nowhere to fall through, but the dried-up husk of the pool still unnerved her. It felt like a desert. Like they had dropped into some upside-down world. Sam waited for Duncan and Caroline, and then the three of them began their descent.

The pool curved smoothly as it sloped down into the deep end. The thick black lines marking off each lane had faded, but Sam could still make them out. She followed the third one, her lucky number. She never lost when she was in lane three, and she hoped that would hold true tonight.

As the walls rose up around her, Sam couldn't help but feel pinned in. The pool seemed so much deeper without the water.

And even though the air pressure hadn't changed, a ringing filled her ears. A sharp pain knifed its way behind her eyes. She held her nose and popped her ears, recalibrating quickly. But it was still an odd sensation, her body acting on its own, responding to memory instead of reality.

Sam glanced up at the walls and read the numbers painted there. Twelve and a half feet. Pretty standard as far as recreational pools went. If she stood on her own shoulders, she wouldn't be able to touch the deck. She wouldn't be able to pull herself to safety.

"Now that we're all here," Bailey said, clearing her throat as she stood on her tiptoes to get everyone's attention. "It's time to get started."

The team roused, coming together to form a circle around Bailey as she took center stage. Sam tried to fade into the background, but everyone kept jostling her, pushing her forward until she ended up right in front. Right where she didn't want to be.

"It's time for a little story," Bailey began, her eyes falling directly on Sam, glinting wickedly in the evening's last light. "A story about a girl who loved the water. Who swam every day, until something tragic happened."

A sudden chill swept through the pool. It tousled hair and ruffled T-shirts. It sent a shiver down Sam's spine as she listened to Bailey's words. As her thoughts raced into the past, recalling the lake's murky water and the reeds' viselike grip on her ankle. The pain in her chest. Kasey trapped underwater beside her. The whole world fading, turning into that empty, fathomless void.

She closed her eyes and tried to breathe. Tried to forget. She couldn't let Bailey see her worked up. She couldn't give the girl that kind of ammunition. That kind of satisfaction.

But she couldn't relax either. And she couldn't get those images out of her head. She didn't know what to do. She thought she'd conquered those memories. That she'd left them way behind. She thought they couldn't hurt her anymore. But with her heart drumming against her rib cage and a cold sweat trickling down her neck, obviously, she'd been wrong.

"Now, you might be wondering why I'm bringing this up tonight." Bailey paused, but no one raised a voice. No one moved as a cloud blew in front of the moon and the pool dropped into complete shadow.

"Well . . ." Bailey drew it out, reveling in the moment, in having everyone's rapt attention. "The girl was on our team. And she died right here. In lane three. Exactly where Sam is standing."

CHAPTER
FIVE

Sam's eyes flashed open and her heart skipped a beat when she saw Bailey pointing at the spot directly underneath her feet. She scrambled backward, searching the ground for physical evidence. For a bloodstain or body imprint.

But there was nothing there. Of course. If the girl had died in the pool, then she would have drowned, not been bludgeoned to death. The water would have washed it all away.

"Scary, isn't it?" Bailey purred.

And Sam's attention snapped back to her captain. To the taunting smile she had plastered on her lips.

"The team used to practice here," Bailey went on. "They'd put a bubble up so they could swim through the fall and winter."

Sam glanced overhead, imagining what it would have looked like back then. The inflated dome blocking out the sky.

The curving plastic ceiling and too-warm temperature making it like they were trapped inside a hot-air balloon.

"Now, though, they call it the graveyard pool."

"I don't remember any of that," someone called out from behind, and Sam snuck a peek over her shoulder, sure the voice had belonged to Caroline. "That's just a stupid urban legend you made up."

"Are you sure about that?" Bailey fired back with more confidence than Sam liked to hear.

"Of course," Caroline said as she stepped forward, confirming that she was indeed the one who had spoken up. She shot her brother a look, but he only smirked and kept his leaning position against the wall, enjoying the festivities too much to step in. Rolling her eyes, Caroline explained it slowly, talking like she would to a toddler. "They closed this pool because the high school's opened up. There's no shocking mystery in that."

"Well, my sister would beg to differ," Bailey replied in a sickly-sweet singsong voice. "Because it happened ten years ago. When she was on the team. I even went to the funeral. Missy was her best friend."

This got everyone's attention. It sucked them all in closer. Sam tried to resist the pull, afraid of what would happen if she let Bailey's whirlpool overcome her. But her story had struck a nerve. Had hit close to her own heart. Her own past.

Flashes of murky water rose up over her head. Slimy tendrils slithered across her legs. Her lungs contracted and squeezed tight. An underwater scream echoed through her ears as the ground swayed underneath her feet, throwing her off-balance, threatening to undo everything she'd worked for, to reveal her as weak in front of her newest adversary. But she couldn't let that happen. She couldn't give Bailey the upper hand.

Sam blinked and willed herself into the present. She pushed the soles of her feet into the ground and steadied herself. She opened her eyes and breathed.

"I remember my sister cried for weeks," Bailey said, still caught up in her story. "She quit the team and vowed never to go back in the water again. Because it wasn't just that Missy had drowned. It was that Missy was the fastest swimmer on the team. One of the fastest in the state. If something like that could happen to her . . . then it could happen to anyone."

Lightning sparked in Bailey's eyes as a sneer lit up her face. Around her, the pool crackled as people shifted uncomfortably, murmuring to each other, corroborating facts, asking if anyone else had heard the story. Sam didn't know what to think—other than that she wanted to get the hell out of there. It was too close to her own near-death experience. To losing Kasey. And even though she'd managed to calm herself down, pulling herself back from the brink, her heart still raced in her chest.

"It's hard to get over something like that." Bailey pushed past the whispering, grabbing everyone's attention again. "My sister was there the day Missy drowned. She tried to save her.

Almost drowned herself. But there was nothing she could do. She said it was like Missy had been dragged down by some invisible force that wouldn't let go. Like a ghost."

A sinking sensation tugged at Sam's stomach, and she couldn't help wondering if Bailey somehow knew about her own past. About the lake. It was impossible, but also, it all felt so targeted. So specifically meant to freak her out. And the worst part was that it was working.

"Why should we care about what happened ten years ago?" Caroline's voice rose again, the only one on the team who seemed to care about reason. But Sam also wondered if Caroline could see her distress. If she was speaking out because she knew Sam needed it. "What's it got to do with us?"

Bailey paused as she considered the question. She took a few measured steps around the deep end, tapping her chin as if truly thinking over her answer. But it was all a show. A bunch of dramatics that, thanks to Caroline, Sam was starting to see through now.

"That's what I thought," Caroline said, filling the interlude, her words smug enough to get a few chuckles out of their teammates.

But Bailey was undeterred. She stopped pacing and whirled around, her hand held high to pull everyone's attention back to her.

"I thought we could all use the history lesson. A reminder of the terrible things that can happen—even to the best swimmers."

She smiled then, her eyes boring into Sam, her finger pointing right at her chest so that everyone knew exactly who she was calling out.

"The water can't be tamed. Not completely. There's always danger. Always something lurking underneath. Something ready to swallow us whole if we aren't careful."

Sam knew Bailey was full of crap. But still—

She took a step back and gulped. She tried to shake the memories out of her head, but she couldn't quite get rid of them. She closed her eyes, but when she did, she could feel that void opening up around her. The suffocation. Her life slipping away with each passing second. She could sense Kasey drifting beside her, sinking down into the murky depths. Trapped in that darkness. Lost to the world. Disappearing forever. All while Sam was helpless to do anything. Was destined to join her.

"Sam? Sam? Are you okay?" someone whispered, shaking her shoulder.

Sam opened her eyes, blinking woozily as if she'd been asleep. Caroline had made her way through the crowd and was standing right next to her, concern etched in the creases of her forehead.

"I'm fine—"

But before Sam could get it all out, a gasp pierced the night. Everyone turned to Bailey, thinking the girl must have seen the cops or an actual ghost. But she only stood there frozen, her arm outstretched, still pointing directly at Sam.

Silence rushed in to fill the empty space left by Bailey's outburst, and everyone shifted to get a better look at Sam. Their eyeballs crawled over her. Studied her. Judged her. She could hear their breathing in the sudden stillness of the night. Could hear the first drops of rain plunking against the bottom of the pool.

Only, it wasn't rain.

"Your nose."

The first voice came out as a whisper. But the refrain grew louder as everyone realized what had happened. What was still happening.

Too late, Sam felt the warm dribble sliding over her lip. She tasted iron in the back of her throat. She narrowed her eyes and glanced down the tip of her nose. Saw the bright red beads of her own blood—drip, drip, dripping—pattering against the dry bottom of the pool.

"Oh!"

Sam clapped her hand over her face, but the damage was already done. She kept her eyes on her feet, avoiding everyone's stares, watching as the droplets of blood collected in a shallow pool underneath her.

"Cursed," Bailey murmured, loud enough for everyone to hear.

Sam's eyebrows shot up. Her head started to spin, and her stomach began churning. She didn't know if it'd be better or worse to throw up right there. The smell, at least, would drive everyone away. Would keep them from staring. It didn't really matter, though. The mortification was done. Bailey had succeeded. She had plenty of ammunition to use against Sam now. It wouldn't take much to turn the team against her. To make them all believe she was the weird new girl who freaked out over silly ghost stories. A scaredy-cat. A loser.

"Back off," Caroline shouted, her voice a buoy bringing Sam up for air. "Give her space to breathe."

Caroline was hovering over Sam, shielding her from view. She looked ready to attack. To take on the whole team if that was what it took.

"You all act like you've never seen a nosebleed before," she went on. "We're in chlorine for, like, three hours a day. Our bodies get dry. Don't act like this hasn't ever happened to you."

Bailey tsked and opened her mouth, but Caroline shut her down immediately.

"And don't even start with that *cursed* stuff. No one is cursed. No one drowned here. You made that up and we *all* know it."

"I guess we'll see," Bailey purred, but after Caroline's defense, no one seemed as interested. The night's spell had been broken and everyone was clearly ready to go.

They milled around the deep end and then eventually made their way back up the pool's slope, where they used the ladders to climb out. Bailey looked after them hopefully, as if she could reel them back in and extend her torture session. But no one turned around. It didn't really matter because she'd gotten what she'd wanted. And she knew it. With a skip in her step, she moved to join Clark, wrapping her hands around his arm as they made their exit together. As they left Caroline and Sam and Duncan alone in the deep end without another thought.

"I don't know where she gets off," Caroline ranted, and Sam found an odd comfort in it. She almost wished someone would mess with Caroline so that she'd have the chance to repay her, to show that she would stick up for her, too.

"Here," Duncan said. He had a packet of tissues in his hand, which he offered to her.

"You two are the best," Sam murmured, because she didn't know what else to say. "Thank you. Both."

She took the tissues and wiped her face. The blood had already started to dry, but she wadded one up and shoved it in her nose for good measure. She glanced down at the bottom of the pool and saw the red puddle. She traced the path it had already started to make down to the very bottom of the pool. Following the trail, she did her best to clean it. If only to hide any evidence that it had happened. She crouched and crawled and had most of it mopped up when she got to where her blood disappeared into the drain.

With a clean tissue, she lifted the grate and swiped under its edge. But when she did, an odd twinkle caught her eye. Pulling the drain cover a little higher, Sam bent closer. She squinted and made out something dull but shiny. It glinted almost imperceptibly in the moonlight, piquing her curiosity. Without thinking too much about it, she reached in and grabbed it, jiggling it a few times until something finally snapped and it came loose.

Sam started to pull the object out, but she jerked back when a silvery snake fell away, slithering back into the drain. Only, it hadn't been an actual reptile. It'd been a chain. The links of a necklace. Which meant that the thing Sam had in her hand must be a charm. Something lost and long forgotten, by the looks of it. Sam held it in her palm and tried to make out what it was supposed to be. It looked like a simple circle. But on closer inspection, she could see that the charm was made up of delicate leaf details swirling together, looping to create what might have been a crown. She couldn't be sure, but she had an idea of what it might be.

"Are you ready?"

Sam startled as Caroline's question snuck up on her. She closed her fist around the charm and slipped it into her pocket with the used tissues. She could clean it off and examine it when she got home. Figure out for sure what it was meant to be.

"Yeah," Sam said, getting back to her feet and turning to face her two new friends. "Let's go. This place gives me the creeps."

CHAPTER
SIX

Cold seeped into Sam's bones, chilling her muscles even though she'd been in the pool for over an hour. No matter how fast she went, she couldn't seem to outswim the shock of that first plunge. She didn't know what was wrong. If the water temperature was unusually cold, or if it was all in her head. Or maybe it was the vibes coming off Bailey, her frigidness seeping into the lane, freezing everyone out.

Sam turned and pushed off into clear water, leaving the wall as Bailey came into view. While Bailey had mostly kept up on the first day of practice, she had fallen behind this morning, dragging at least three arm's lengths back, completely out of touch. Which was how Sam liked it. After the stunt Bailey had pulled last night, there was no way Sam was going to let her come close. She could make fun of Sam all she wanted, tell everyone that she was a freak and that she was cursed or whatever, but she couldn't outswim her. So, she couldn't win.

Putting her head down, Sam chugged along. She flipped in the deep end and headed back for the set's final twenty-five. She focused on her arms as they powered through the water. She counted her strokes and turned her head to breathe every third one, the familiar rhythm working to calm her racing thoughts, to bring her back to equilibrium. She couldn't let Bailey get in her head. Couldn't let her disrupt her training. She had a goal. She'd moved here for a reason. She wouldn't let Bailey become a distraction. The pool had been her safe place for as long as she could remember. She wouldn't let her new nemesis take that away.

With a final push, Sam lunged into the wall. She pulled her feet under her and stood up, lifting her goggles to her forehead as she caught her breath. In the next lane, she could hear the boys whooping and hollering. Glancing over, she saw them bunched up along one of the lane lines, keeping the center clear so that everyone could finish into the wall. They were jumping up and down, giving each other high fives and chest bumps, acting silly and rambunctious—like a bunch of sixteen-year-olds. It was kind of contagious, all that energy buzzing among them, and Sam couldn't help but smile.

However, as the last boy came swimming in, something shifted. Their smiles twisted into smirks. Their eyes darted back and forth, an impish, knowing exchange. And then, as if a signal had been flashed, they pounced.

One of them grabbed the swimmer's ankles and yanked them back hard, while another tugged at his suit and then smacked his butt. The sharp sound echoed off the pool's high ceiling. The boys' hooting and hollering grew even louder as the swimmer jumped up, his face red and raw with embarrassment and indignation. He tried to dance out of their reach, but they outnumbered him with their slaps and laughs and grunts.

In another situation, it could have been seen as rough-housing. As boys will be boys. But here—right now—Sam understood the awful cruelty in it. Especially when she finally saw who their target was.

"Coach!" Duncan exclaimed, his hands raised to cover his chest, to protect against more attacks.

"Come on now," Coach Hendricks replied from the deck, his eyes glued to his clipboard, purposely avoiding the scene. "It's just a little teasing. Now get back out there and finish up the set."

Sam couldn't see Duncan's eyes through his tinted goggles, but she'd bet they were rolling into the back of his head. Or shooting death-ray glares at everyone who had jumped on him. The rest of the boys had already moved on, though, sneaking self-satisfied smiles with each other as they set off for their last two hundred. Sam didn't understand how they could be so mean. Or why Coach Hendricks didn't step in and say something.

"More like harassing me," Duncan muttered as he laid his head back in the water and pushed off the wall.

"Nice work today," Coach Hendricks said, turning to give Sam a cheesy thumbs-up. He tapped his pen on his clipboard, where he'd undoubtedly written out her splits for each of the morning's sets. "Keep this up and you'll be breaking records."

Sam replied with a weak smile, her stomach suddenly queasy. Right now she just wanted to get to the cooldown. To get out of there. Luckily, as the rest of the girls in her lane finished up, they did just that.

Swimming the last few laps, Sam took it easy, stretching her arms long, letting the water linger on her fingertips and palms. She relaxed into it, allowing the slow pace to unwind her muscles and calm her mind. She didn't care about finishing first. This was the one time that Bailey could lap her and it wouldn't mean a thing.

As she swam, Sam snuck glances over at the other lane, checking in on Duncan, seeing if anyone else was bothering him. The boys seemed to have moved on. No one pinched or prodded or poked him as he went about his cooldown. But the casual cruelty from earlier worried Sam. It infuriated her. Made her think that this kind of thing happened more often than not. It was different when girls and boys bullied one another, the things they picked on, the tactics they used. But it was devastating all the same. There were so many ways to get under someone's skin. So many ways to make them feel different and horrible. Sam wished things could be easier. For herself and Duncan. For Caroline, too. They had each other's backs, but was that enough?

Completing her workout, Sam held up. She fiddled with her goggles and took off her cap. She ran her fingers through her tangled hair as the pool emptied out. As she waited for Duncan to drag himself onto the deck.

"Are they always like that?" she asked, getting right to the point once Duncan was beside her. "I mean, Clark and the rest of them."

While Caroline's brother hadn't been the main instigator in the boys' lane, he'd overseen it all. He was the captain. He held a power of influence. If he said something, the other boys would back off. They'd listen to him. The fact that he hadn't made him complicit.

Duncan looked at Sam for a few seconds, his eyes heavy and red. Or maybe that was just from his goggles.

"It's fine," he eventually replied. "I'm fine. They've been like that since I came out as gay. I guess I'm an easy target. But I can take care of myself. It's not that bad."

"But you really should talk to someone. Report them or—"

"What good would that do?" Duncan cut her off. "Coach Hendricks isn't going to step in. You saw how he handled it."

"What about the principal? Or another teacher? Your parents?"

"That would only make things worse," Duncan sighed. "They'd get a slap on the wrist, if that. And then they'd just keep doing what they've always done. Only they'd go in on me harder."

"But you can't—"

"Trust me." Duncan looked sincere as he held Sam's shaking hands. As he delivered his truth. "It's easier this way. As long as I don't make waves, I can keep my head above water."

Sam didn't like the sound of that. She didn't agree with it at all. She started to shake her head, but Duncan was having none of it.

"You have enough on your plate with Bailey. Watch out for yourself. You don't need to worry about me."

With that, Duncan dropped Sam's hands and headed toward the locker room. She turned to keep after him, but something splashed behind her. She whirled around and found that her water bottle had tipped over and fallen into the pool. She stooped and fished it out, making sure that her necklace was still there, looped around the spout of the bottle, where she'd left it during practice.

She unclasped it, then hooked it around her neck. She fingered Kasey's seashell and then picked up the new charm she'd found in the graveyard pool the night before. After going home and rubbing it down with some baking soda and soap, she'd managed to get most of the shine back and seen that it was exactly what she'd thought—a silver laurel wreath, the symbol of ancient Olympic champions. An auspicious discovery.

Clutching it now, the edges of the tiny leaves dug into Sam's finger, almost sharp enough to draw blood. And then a whimper of laughter trickled into her ears. Followed by a cannonball splash. A bloodcurdling scream.

Sam blinked, her pulse racing, the hair on her arms standing straight up. Her eyes swept over the pool in front of her, but it sat undisturbed, not a soul in sight, not a wave rippling the placid surface. She shook her head as if she had water trapped in her ears and hurried out of there.

Pushing into the locker room, Sam picked up snatches of the conversations swirling around her. Some were about boys and some were about homework assignments. Some were even about her—her nosebleed, how scared she'd looked last night in the graveyard pool, the fact that she was faster than Bailey. Sam tried to ignore those whispers, knowing they were coming from Paige, the girl who'd already made her dislike of Sam known on the first day of practice, and all the others who seemed to hang on every mean word that Bailey had to say. Sam didn't have time for them. Which made her realize that maybe she wasn't so different from Duncan. Maybe she also knew a thing or two about ignoring the bullies in order to keep her head above water.

Making it to her locker, Sam spun through her combination, lifting her feet as she realized that someone had spilled water all over the floor. It annoyed her—even though she was already wet—because she knew it'd likely been done on purpose. Another small thing to get under her skin. To make her feel uncomfortable and unwelcome. Well, she wasn't going to give in so easily. Bailey and her army of minions would have to step up their game if they planned to scare her off. With a click, Sam's lock popped and the door swung open.

The smell hit her first, an odor so noxious that she gagged on the spot. The rotten, sour stench filled her nostrils and made her head spin. She clamped her fingers over her nose and pinched it shut, using her palm to cover her mouth, to keep herself from vomiting.

Cautiously, she peeked into the locker, gagging again as she took in the carnage, the blood and guts and brains oozing everywhere. The pile of severed fish heads glistened, their unseeing eyes dim yet gazing up at her all the same. She met their stares. Saw the haunting look of death and decay locked within them. The hopelessness. Then she turned and ran, distancing herself from the chorus of laughter that had erupted around her, from the mean girls who had planned it all, who were bent on making her life miserable.

CHAPTER
SEVEN

Sam sat on the cold tile floor, shivering in a pool of her own making. Her wet suit clung to her body, pinching her chest in like a straitjacket. She tilted her head back and tried to breathe. Tried to visualize happy, soothing thoughts.

But all she could see were those dead fish heads, the blood and gore of their rotting flesh, their slimy, scaly skin and gasping mouths. Their foul odor was imprinted on her nostrils, tangled in her hair, tainting the taste buds on her tongue.

She sucked up all the moisture in her mouth and tried to spit it out, tried to blow her nose clean. But the smell lingered. The other girls' laughter echoed in her head. Death and decay wrapped her in their embrace. Cursed her. Because even though Sam didn't believe that story about Missy, this was a kind of curse on its own. Bailey was her demon. Her tormentor. And she had no clue how to exorcise her.

"There you are."

Sam whipped her head up as Caroline came around the corner. She had a towel bundled under one arm, which she unfurled and draped over Sam's shoulders. Then she plopped down on the floor right next to her.

"You'll get wet," Sam mumbled, scooting away from Caroline in a hurry, trying to mop up her puddle.

"I'll dry." Caroline slid in, closing the distance Sam had opened.

"But—"

"I'm not worried about it," Caroline insisted. "I'm worried about you."

Sam didn't know how to respond, so she sat there quietly, refusing to meet Caroline's gaze. She pulled the towel tighter around her shoulders and shifted uncomfortably. She was embarrassed. And angry. Furious at Bailey, but also at herself. It was a terrible prank, disgusting and foul and cruel, but Sam should have been able to handle it. She shouldn't have lost her cool like that. She shouldn't have turned her back and run away. When she'd fled that locker room, she'd lost. She'd let Bailey win. She didn't know how to explain it to Caroline, but she couldn't keep ignoring her. She couldn't keep her new friend hanging.

"Do I smell bad?" she asked.

Caroline's eyes narrowed in confusion, but she played along, leaning in and taking a whiff.

"I'm getting hints of chlorine. So, nothing out of the ordinary."

"Good," Sam replied shakily. "That's good."

She could feel Caroline's concern, but she couldn't bring herself to turn and face it. Because what if it wasn't that? What if it was pity instead?

"That was awful," Caroline said, a gentleness in her voice, as if Sam were a fawn she didn't want to scare off. "I can't believe that Bailey would do something so—so mean."

"So, it was her, right?" Sam had assumed that Bailey was behind it, but she appreciated the confirmation.

"She was recording the whole thing on her phone," Caroline said. "Cackling about it with the other girls. I'm so sorry. I should have known she'd do something like this. I should have stepped in and stopped it. Warned you, at least."

"Warned me?"

And now it was Caroline's turn to clam up.

"Is there something else?" Sam asked. "Has Bailey ever bullied you?"

Caroline pursed her lips, her jaw flexing as she clamped it shut. But then, eventually, she relented, and it all came tumbling out. "It wasn't a big deal. But last year, when I was a freshman on the team, she was pretty relentless. It was mostly small stuff. Snide remarks and cold shoulders. She'd soak my towel so that I didn't have anything to use after I showered. She'd empty my water bottle at the beginning of practice. She even hid my clothes a couple of times so that I had to call my mom to drop off new ones."

"Why would she do all that?" Sam asked.

Caroline shrugged.

"I don't know what I did to piss her off, but eventually she started dating my brother and turned all sweet and fake BFF-y with me. That is, until I made it clear that I had no interest in being her friend. Now she just kind of ignores me, which works for both of us."

Sam shook her head, disgusted and confused and mad. She'd seen Clark with the other boys picking on Duncan. Which meant that he was probably just as bad as Bailey. A couple of bullies. Captains and ringleaders. If only they used their positions to bring the team together instead of driving it apart. Because who had that kind of energy to waste on making someone else's life so miserable?

"That's why I try to call her out on her crap," Caroline went on. "I'm the only one who can, at least while she's with my brother. She can't touch me—not really—without losing him."

Sam breathed out and let her head fall against Caroline. She felt her shoulders unwinding, the tension going out of them as she relaxed. She wasn't in this alone. Caroline had come to her defense before, and she appreciated it so much.

"Are you girls all right?" Both Sam and Caroline jumped, turning their heads to see Assistant Coach Carson looking down at them, her hands clasped together, thumbs moving in worried circles. "Did I overhear you saying something about Bailey?"

Sam wanted to explain what Bailey had done. How she had terrorized her with that fish-head prank. Coach Hendricks hadn't done anything when those guys were harassing Duncan, but this was different. And Assistant Coach Carson was a teacher. She'd be on their side. She'd go to the principal and turn Bailey in.

"It was nothing," Caroline jumped in before Sam could speak. "Just talking about how she's been a great captain this year."

"Are you sure?"

Sam wanted to tell the truth, but one glance at Caroline told her that she should leave it. So, she did, nodding her head and plastering on a fake smile that wouldn't have been hard to see through if Assistant Coach Carson was really looking.

"Well, I guess I'll see you in English class later," the assistant coach said, lingering over the words, giving the girls one last opening, which neither took. "If you ever need to talk about anything, you know where to find me. You can always trust me."

"Thanks," Caroline replied. "We'll remember that."

And with a little wave, they watched their coach disappear around the corner.

"Why didn't you tell her what happened?" Sam whispered. "She could have helped us."

"She can't do anything. Not to Bailey Miller. We rat, and

it's only gonna get worse for us. They'll want proof. Her parents will complain. There won't be any real punishment. And then Bailey will come after us looking for revenge."

"But how do you know that?"

"Because it's happened before. Last year, to one of the freshmen on the team. She told the principal about how Bailey was messing with her. Stealing her clothes and slipping vinegar into her water bottle. Spreading nasty rumors about her behind her back. But Bailey got her parents to complain. To say the girl was making it all up. Next thing you know, all of Bailey's friends are taking her side, lying about what really went on. And the girl is being gaslit. Being told that everything Bailey had done to her hadn't actually happened. They were relentless and made her think she was delusional. It got so bad that she ended up transferring to another school."

"But that's not fair."

"It's just how it goes for pretty, popular girls. There's no getting justice. At least, not through the normal channels."

Here, Caroline winked at Sam. Which made Sam wonder if her friend had something planned. If she had her own way of getting back at Bailey. A way that wouldn't get them in trouble.

"Now, let's get you out of that suit. I have some extra clothes you can borrow. I'm assuming everything in your locker is going to smell like dead fish."

CHAPTER
EIGHT

"So, how's practice going?"

Sam looked up from the table, a textbook open in front of her, her homework half-done. Her dad stood at the sink, a towel and plate in hand as he waited for her answer.

"It's been good."

She knew he was trying to make conversation, but what else could she say? She saw him talking to Coach Hendricks every morning when he dropped her off. Checking in on her progress. Offering suggestions for sets and drills. He'd been an athlete in college—he would have gone pro if a blown-out knee hadn't ended his football career—but he'd never been a swimmer. That hadn't stopped him from reading up on it, though. From listening to coaching interviews and podcasts. He knew what it took to be an elite athlete. The grueling training program. The meal plans and sleep schedules. The unwavering drive. The dedication. The support system and sacrifice. And he always had ideas on how to make her faster, which he wasn't afraid to voice.

"And how are the other girls?"

"The other girls?"

Sam repeated his words back to him so that she'd have time to think. She knew her dad didn't care about the other girls on a personal level. On whether they were nice and welcoming. On if she'd made any friends. He only cared about them in relation to how they affected her training. Could they keep up? Were they fast enough to push her, to make her better?

So how could she tell him about what was really going on? Best case, he'd tell her to suck it up. To push through the pranks and mean comments. That the adversity would make her stronger. Make her tougher. Make her race ready. Worst case, he'd go to Coach Hendricks himself. Then Sam would be the girl who couldn't deal. Who couldn't solve her own problems. She'd be the one relying on her dad to swoop in and save her, which would kind of undermine everything he'd taught her about resilience and self-reliance in the first place.

"They're good," Sam lied, keeping it simple, knowing that if she said more she'd say too much. She wanted to show him that she could handle things on her own. And besides, she didn't need to add any more stress to his life, not when he was looking for a job and trying to manage the pain that still flared up from his old injury.

It had been a week since the fish head incident, and in that week, Bailey had mostly left Sam alone. But Sam still felt uneasy every time Bailey was around. She had to be on her guard. She could hold her own one-on-one if it came down to it, but Bailey had practically the whole team on her side. And Sam couldn't risk them banding together against her. Not after what Caroline had told her about the freshman the year before. The girl who'd gotten bullied so badly that she'd quit swimming and changed schools. What if Bailey and her minions told Coach Hendricks that Sam was the one making trouble? What if he believed their lies and she got kicked off the team? Where would she be then? And what would her dad say? She couldn't be yet another disappointment in his life. She couldn't be anything less than his shining swimming champion.

Sam just had to put her head down and endure it. Which she could do. However, it didn't help that Bailey liked to replay her little prank video every chance she got. Even though it didn't seem like she'd sent it out to anyone—because that would be too incriminating—she cued it up for her friends after practice or during lunch, and Sam would have to listen to her own gagging coming through the grainy audio, the cackling laughter following her frenzied locker room exit. But then, at the end, she'd hear Caroline's shouts. A muffling as her hand pushed Bailey's phone away, trying to smash it when she realized what the girl had done. And that gave Sam comfort. It was an ending she would have cut out of the video and played on a loop if she could. A reminder that she wasn't alone on the team. That she didn't have to put up with Bailey and all the other girls by herself.

"I talked to Coach Hendricks." Sam's dad's voice cut through her thoughts, bringing her back to the kitchen and his original question. "He said you're looking great. Working hard. Shaving off seconds. Getting closer to our goals."

Sam's lips puckered at that. At the way he said *our*, as if he were in the pool swimming the laps with her. But he didn't seem to notice as he plowed right on.

"Don't forget that's why we're here. It's me and your mom's investment in you. In giving you the opportunity to get to the next level. State records. College scholarships. Olympic trials. It's all right there for you to take if you work hard enough. And the opportunity only comes along once. So don't waste it. Trust me. Or you'll live to regret it."

Sam bit her bottom lip and swallowed down her nerves. She spotted the way her dad grimaced, either because a pain had twitched in his knee or because he was remembering his own glory days. His potential. The what-could-have-been if he hadn't gotten hurt. She knew how much he had wanted that life. Athletic stardom. And how much it had crushed him when all that hard work had slipped out of reach. Her dad had poured everything into her. He thought so highly of her. Wanted so much for her.

And Sam wanted it, too. She did. But the pressure to excel could be hard to manage at times. She couldn't disappoint him, though. She knew that. Failure was not an option. Not in their household. Not with everything her parents had given up for her and her dream.

"We have an intersquad meet coming up next week," Sam said, only now remembering Coach Hendricks's announcement at the end of practice. "It's just like a scrimmage, but it'll be a good measure of where my times are."

"Well!" Her dad clapped his hands together, a gleeful glint in his eyes. "That's what I'm talking about. I expect you'll be fast. Finish first."

"I always do."

Sam knew this was what he wanted to hear. And since it was the truth, she didn't feel bad saying it. Bailey had started to come up on her a little bit in practice, but she was still only nipping at Sam's toes. Not fast enough for Sam to worry. As much crap as Bailey talked in the locker room, she would never be able to touch Sam when it came down to what really mattered. To the pool and a race to the finish.

On the table beside her, Sam's phone lit up.

"It's Mom," she said, glancing at her dad for permission to take it.

"Go," he said, shooing her out of the room. "But homework after."

Sam barely listened as she swiped her phone off the table

and padded out of the kitchen. Once she was out of the room, she answered.

"How are you doing, honey?" Sam's mom asked as soon as the video call had connected.

"Everything's great." Sam was surprised at how easily the lie slipped out. She was getting good at it. But, she reasoned, almost everything was great. Everything that didn't include Bailey. "I've missed you."

"And I've missed you," Sam's mom echoed. "I can't wait until my next visit."

Sam paused as she did the math. "Two weeks?"

Her mom nodded. "It'll be here before you know it."

Sam swallowed down her disappointment. She couldn't let her mom see. This was one of the investments that her dad had talked about. A sacrifice, really. When her dad had lost his job and they'd moved, her mom had stayed behind, working until she could find a new job in Wentworth. It was a four-hour drive, so she was only able to come up every two or three weeks. But Sam couldn't wait for the day when she'd be able to join them for good. When they would all be back together again under the same roof.

"So how are things going?" Sam's mom asked. "What's new with you?"

"Just lots of swimming," Sam replied, not realizing she'd sighed when she'd said it.

"And you're okay with that? You still like swimming, right?"

The question caught Sam off guard. It didn't come up often, and her mom was the only one who ever asked her. And only when her dad wasn't around to hear.

"Of course." Sam rushed to answer, worried that she'd already taken too long.

Because what was she without swimming? Who was she? And hadn't her parents sacrificed so much for her? Her mom living away from them now? All the practices and meets her dad had driven her to over the years? Every weekend sucked up by what she was so good at? What she could maybe be the best at, if she put in the work?

"Well, I just don't want you burning out. If it ever gets to be too much, you can tell us. Me or your dad. Sometimes I worry that we put too much pressure on you. That we made the wrong decision—"

"It's fine, Mom. I'm fine. I promise. Swimming's great. I'm getting faster. I'm making friends. It's all good. This was the right decision."

It had to be. And Sam would make sure of it. Because there was no going back now. She wouldn't disappoint her family. Wouldn't let her dad down. She wouldn't let them waste their time and energy and money on her.

"I've got to finish up some homework," Sam said, suddenly ready to wrap things up. A guilty weight settled in her stomach. But it was for the best. She didn't want her mom to worry about her. Not on top of everything else. "Love you."

"Love you, too."

And then they hung up, leaving Sam with a restless, heavy feeling that made it hard for her to breathe. Instead of heading back to the kitchen to finish her homework, she pivoted and walked down the hallway, closing the door to the bathroom behind her. She turned the tap and let it run until it was warm. Then she plugged the drain.

As the water began to fill the tub, Sam turned to look at her reflection in the mirror. Seeing her puffy, red eyes, she realized just how exhausted she was. Morning practices were no joke, both the waking up early and the workouts themselves. But a new soreness crept through her shoulders. Her abs. Her quads. It was a welcome ache. One that meant she was getting stronger. That she and her dad and her mom weren't wasting anything.

The water glugged away behind Sam, and she started to relax. Her chest opened as the restlessness from before lifted. The new charm on her necklace winked at her, made her feel confident. It reminded her that she was a champion. That she was meant to win.

She listened as the water ran through its descending scale, lowering in pitch as the bath grew deeper. The steam had already begun to fog up the mirror, wiping her reflection away. She rolled her neck from side to side and raised her arms over her head. She let the stretch sink into every muscle in her body.

When she could tell the tub was close to full, she turned, ready to dip her fingers in, to test the warmth before the plunge. But what she saw froze her in place. A chill ran through her, one that could have iced over the steamed-up mirror and cracked it into a thousand razor-sharp shards. She stuttered backward, her hip colliding with the counter, her hand flying to her mouth. What she was looking at wasn't possible. It couldn't be real. The color was all wrong. The thick, crimson stream pouring from the tap and pooling in the tub couldn't have come from their pipes. It was terrible, like something straight out of a horror movie. A vampire's supper. Or the place where a serial killer finished off his victims.

The bloody bath continued to glug, continued to fill, threatening to spill over the rim of the tub. With some of the shock wearing off, Sam leapt into action. She shut off the tap. And then, without thinking, she plunged her hand into the crimson murk, groping for the plug, trying to rip it loose.

But as she tugged on it, something grabbed hold of her wrist. It yanked her down toward the water. She cried out and scrambled on the floor, keeping her head up, tucking her legs underneath her so that she could brace herself against the side of the tub. She pulled, pressing with her legs, straining with every muscle in her body, and finally the hold loosened. The plug ripped free. Her body flung itself backward as the resistance disappeared and she found herself against the counter again.

She sat on the floor, clutching the bathtub stopper to her chest, breathing hard and fast as she listened to the water swirling down the drain, as the red tendrils of blood got sucked into oblivion.

When it had finished, Sam got up slowly. She cautiously peeked over the lip of the tub, expecting to see a bloodbath, the aftermath of a murder. But it was squeaky clean, the tub slick with a sheen of fresh, clear water.

Sam glanced down at her hand and the bath stopper in it. She examined the wet spots on her shirt. But it was all clean, too. Not a drop of red in sight.

Her hands shook as she took it all in. As her brain tried to process what it'd seen with the proof that was there in front of her now.

Was she really that tired? Were the early mornings getting to her that badly?

Or had Bailey's pranks gotten that elaborate? Sam glanced over to the window, but she didn't see anyone there. And if it were a prank, where had the blood gone?

Sam thought about Bailey and the story of that girl who'd drowned. Missy. *A curse. A ghost.* But Bailey had made all that up, Caroline had said.

Sam blinked a few times and glared at the tub, willing the blood to return. At least then she'd know she wasn't seeing things. That she hadn't made it all up.

But nothing changed.

And nothing would change.

Sam chastised herself for freaking out—whether it was another prank or just her silly imagination, it wasn't worth the distraction. She needed to get some sleep. To relax and stop worrying.

With a final sigh, Sam picked herself up from the floor. She flicked off the bathroom light and headed toward her room, her eyes starting to droop, the tiredness hitting her before she'd made it halfway down the hallway. She paused for a second and yawned. And as she did, she felt something strange underfoot. A wet spot, like someone had spilled a drink on the carpet. Soaked it through. She backed up and bent over, tilting her head to get a better angle.

And then she spotted it. A trail running from the bathroom all the way to her room. Footprints. Dark and wet. Smaller than her own.

The chill from before crept over Sam again, and she was suddenly wide awake, her heart drumming against her rib cage. Her gaze swept over the footprints, back and forth and back and forth. And this time she knew she wasn't seeing things. She wasn't making it up. But as hell-bent as Bailey was on getting to her, she couldn't possibly have gone so far as to break into Sam's home, could she?

The thought needled at Sam. It infuriated her. Because Bailey *would* go that far. She'd dumped a bucketful of fish heads in her locker, hadn't she? She'd do anything to get under

Sam's skin, to distract her from training, to try to scare her off. But Sam wouldn't let her win.

With a new determination simmering in her gut, Sam leapt into action. She forgot about the bathtub and the wet footprints. She rushed to her room and grabbed her laptop, opening a new tab and typing: *Wentworth Public Park + Drowning.*

She'd get to the bottom of Bailey's little ghost story. She'd prove to everyone that the girl was a liar.

CHAPTER
NINE

The table rocked underneath them. Sam's bagel sat in front of her, smeared with cream cheese and untouched on its Styrofoam plate, while her orange juice threatened to spill over. She tried to steady her shaking leg, but she couldn't calm down. She was too excited, bursting with what she'd found out the night before.

"Everything okay?" Caroline asked, glancing over her shoulder at the table where Bailey and Clark were sitting erupted with laughter. "Did something happen?"

Caroline's lips drew down into a frown, a worried look, but Sam quickly shook her head, not wanting her friend to get the wrong idea.

"It's just something I wanted to tell you about. Well, you and Duncan. Where is he?"

Caroline shrugged as she picked at her own bagel. "You know how he is."

"Late?" Sam offered.

"Yeah. But usually for a good reason."

As if he'd been waiting for a cue, Duncan stomped into the room, lugging his swim bag over one shoulder. His hair was still wet, like he'd just gotten out of the shower, and Sam knew it must be making him livid. Something must have happened for him to come out like this. Something really bad. When he got to their table, he pulled his bag off and threw it on the floor, collapsing into the seat next to Sam.

"What happened to you?" Caroline yelped, dropping her half-eaten bagel as Duncan huffed and stormed in his chair.

"Some idiot—"

Duncan shot a sideways glare at the table where Clark and the other boys sat with Bailey. Sam could tell they were listening in, waiting for Duncan's reaction, for an explosion.

"Some idiot"—Duncan lowered his voice, his jaw locked in a grimace—"decided it'd be funny to break into my locker. To take my clothes and string them up for everyone to see. My socks and shirt. My pants. My underwear—"

Here, Duncan cut off, gulping. His cheeks burned so red that Sam could feel the heat hitting her own face.

"Do you know how humiliating it is? Having to listen to them make their stupid comments about tighty-whities? Like they don't know the difference between Hanes and Calvin Klein."

The seconds ticked by, and Sam held her breath, waiting

for her friend to either blow up or melt down into a puddle. It was more of what he'd already been putting up with. More belittling and bullying. More poking and prodding and pestering. And no one was doing anything about it.

"Yo, Duncan!" A boy at Clark's table had gotten to his feet and shouted across the room, making sure that everyone on the team was listening. "I've got an extra pair of underwear if you need them. I swear they're clean."

And then he pulled back his arm and threw something their way, the projectile unfurling and fluttering like a bird coming in for a landing, and falling neatly in the middle of their table.

"They're called boxers," the boy went on. "They're super comfy. Manlier than what you've got on."

There were more snickers, and Sam's stomach clenched as she saw Duncan sink deeper into his chair, his face a brilliant, sunburned red.

"Why don't you grow up."

Sam surprised even herself as she shot to her feet. She snatched the boxers off the table and hurled them back.

It only made everyone howl louder, though, as the boy who'd thrown them in the first place started imitating her, stomping his foot and putting his hands on his hips like a child in the middle of a tantrum. He mimed her throwing motion, but did so with an exaggerated, limp wrist, playing it up for his crew, getting more and more laughs with each pass. There was nothing Sam could do but sit back down . . . and retreat.

"I hate them," she seethed.

"Keith is the worst," Caroline agreed.

"And your brother," Sam shot back.

"I've tried talking to Clark." Caroline sighed as if this was a long-standing grievance of hers. "I've tried convincing him and the other guys to lay off. But he doesn't listen to me. He doesn't care what I think."

"Well, somebody should do something about them."

Sam glared at Clark's table, glowering at Keith as he elbowed his neighbors and hammed it up. He had a smug grin on his face. A self-satisfied look that burrowed underneath her skin. What did he have to be proud of? He should be ashamed. He should be afraid.

As the thought popped into Sam's head, she felt something in the air shift. She turned back to her table and noticed that Duncan's hands had balled into fists. A serious scowl had settled over his mouth.

"He'll get what's coming to him," Caroline said, squeezing Duncan's hand, holding on until he relaxed.

"Hopefully sooner than later," Duncan sighed, his anger deflating with each exhaled breath, his whole body shrinking.

"Eat something," Sam said, pushing her bagel across the table. "Anger on an empty stomach only leads to trouble."

Duncan grimaced but picked up the food. He took a bite and chewed slowly, cautiously, keeping his eye out in case the boys might have something else planned for him. It must have been exhausting, having to be on guard at all times. Having to always look over his shoulder. Sam could relate, though. After everything that Bailey had thrown at her, she didn't trust anything. The girl could and would do anything to bother her. To throw her off. She was relentless.

"So, what was it that you wanted to tell us?" Caroline asked, bringing Sam back to the moment, back to her earlier excitement. She'd forgotten about what had gotten her so excited. About all the news articles she'd sifted through the night before. Everything she'd read up on. But now it flooded her mind, all the details brimming to get out.

"I found something."

Both Caroline and Duncan looked at her with big, expectant stares.

"I found Missy," Sam clarified. "The girl who drowned at the graveyard pool."

"Wait, what do you mean? That Bailey was telling the truth?" Caroline asked, looking as shocked as Sam had felt when she'd first discovered the articles.

As Sam nodded, she beckoned them to lean in close, dropping her voice so that no one could overhear.

"As much as it pains me to say it, there was at least some truth to the story Bailey told us."

This elicited another glance over to Clark and Bailey's table. To Keith, who'd apparently moved on from his impressions of Sam, spinning his plastic water bottle and pumping it in his fist as he told some new story or joke.

"It's just like Bailey said," Sam went on. "Missy Caplin drowned at the Wentworth Public Pool ten years ago."

The articles online had been clear about a lot of the details. Missy had been a freshman on the high school swim team. A regional champion. Sam had even looked up the girl's times and found that they weren't too far off her own.

"If she was that good, then how'd she drown?" Duncan asked, interrupting Sam's recap.

"That's the strangest part," she explained. "No one really knows. Or, at least, no one is telling. There were a few witnesses, but they all claimed they didn't see anything. It happened after practice one morning."

Sam paused, letting this most interesting part of the story sink in. Because it wasn't what had happened that left her asking questions. It was how. Things didn't add up. Or they shouldn't. Because if they did, if someone as fast as Missy could drown out of nowhere, then no one was safe. Not even Sam.

"There are theories that Missy cramped up. That she was faking it for attention or as a prank and that no one noticed until it was too late. Some people even think she overworked herself. That she was exhausted from her strenuous training regime and her body just gave out."

Sam didn't know which story she believed. They all seemed plausible and impossible at the same time. But the fact that no one had seen anything bothered her. No one had jumped in and tried to save Missy, though Bailey had lied and made it sound like her sister had. It just seemed too unlikely. Too coordinated. There had to be something more.

"And why do we care so much about a girl who drowned ten years ago?" Duncan asked.

"I—don't know." Sam only realized this as she said it. At first, she'd wanted to investigate Missy to prove that Bailey was a liar. That she'd made up the whole story. But as Sam had gotten deeper into the story, she couldn't help but feel a connection with the girl. She'd stumbled onto an old interview with the local paper where Missy had talked about her dreams of breaking state records and swimming in college. Of trying out for the Olympic team.

Wasn't that exactly what Sam wanted? Wasn't that why she was putting up with the morning practices and aching muscles? With the perpetually dry hair and itchy skin? With Bailey?

"I feel bad for her," Sam eventually said. "All that potential and she never got to see it through."

They all fell quiet as Sam's words sank in. As she thought about how it would feel to have her dreams snuffed out, suffocated before she had a chance to realize them.

She jerked upright as a chill blew across the back of her neck. As a voice dripped into her ears, too soft for her to make out. Gone before she could understand.

Avenge me.

An uproar of laughter burst out from Clark and Bailey's table, and Sam turned to see that Keith had grabbed the boxers and put them on his head. He had his water bottle out and was holding it like a microphone, singing into it, serenading Clark with some kind of love song. Out of the corner of her eye, Sam saw Duncan slip lower in his seat. She saw the mortification all over his face, and it made her so mad.

Her fists clenched as blood rushed to her head. She opened her mouth to shout across the room, but before she could go to bat for her friend, a hiss filled the air, loud enough to belong to an anaconda. The hiss swelled, like a kettle of water coming to a rapid boil, and then an explosion rocketed through the room. At the same time, Keith's head jerked back, whiplashing against his shoulder blades and then falling against the table.

A hush fell over the room, tense and unbroken. Everyone's eyes locked on Keith, waiting, worried, confused. Slowly, he lifted his head, his hair falling away from his face. He looked all right. In one piece.

Then a dribble of blood leaked from the corner of his mouth. His lips parted and his two front teeth came tumbling out, rolling across the table like a pair of dice. Someone screamed, and that broke the tenuous calm that had fallen.

Everyone at Keith's table jumped up. They scrambled to get away. By the shocked looks on their faces, no one knew what had happened. But as the commotion continued, Sam heard something soft and distinct under it all, a skittering like a stone across water. She glanced down as something settled against her foot, and she saw an engorged rubber cap, blue and unmistakable, the top to Keith's water bottle.

"Sam!" Caroline gasped, her fingers winding around Sam's wrist, snapping her attention up from the ground. "Your nose."

Caroline wiped at her face, and Sam raised her hand to touch her own upper lip.

The blood was warm and thick. Slippery. She rubbed her fingertips together, thinking as her gaze flitted to the bottle cap and then to Keith, who had started howling, his hysterics making it so that no one glanced her way. That no one noticed the blood dripping from her nose.

Her eyes dropped back to the ruined bottle cap and she bent over to pick it up. She examined it closely, her fingers caressing the rubber, feeling the rounded edges where it had exploded. She didn't know how it could have happened, how it could have flown off like that, but she didn't really care. Keith had gotten exactly what he deserved, and she didn't feel bad for him at all.

CHAPTER
TEN

Cheers rang out around Sam, but she couldn't hear them from the water. She could only see her teammates clapping, their mouths opened wide on the deck as she churned through the pool. Her hand stabbed into the wall and she popped up, staring at the scoreboard—her time displayed there in flashing lights. It wasn't a personal best, but it was pretty close. Not bad for a scrimmage. And she'd beaten everyone else by at least four seconds. She memorized the time, knowing her dad would want to go over it when she got home, and lifted herself out of the pool. She peeled her swim cap off and grabbed a towel. She patted herself dry as a new heat of boys mounted the blocks, ready to dive in.

"How are you so fast?" Caroline asked as she skipped up to Sam and gave her a high five.

"Lots of practice." Sam smiled as she caught her breath,

proving that she wasn't so invincible. She got tired, too. While the two-hundred freestyle was her best event, it was also the most exhausting. The middle distance always took it out of her: too long to be an all-out sprint, but too short to be able to fall into a comfortable pace.

"Are you gonna be ready for the one hundred?" Caroline asked. "That's your last race, right?"

"Yeah," Sam assured her. "I'll be fine. I recover fast."

"Good. Because that's Bailey's race and you have to beat her."

"I'm not worried," Sam said, her confidence pumping her up so that she stood taller. "Bailey's going down."

Caroline clapped and did a little dance, spinning around until she spotted Bailey sitting on a bench off to the side of the pool. She had a parka wrapped around her shoulders, keeping her muscles warm while she waited. Her headphones peeked out from her ears, a serious game-face scowl blanketing her expression.

"She looks ready to tear someone's head off," Caroline joked.

"She'll have to catch up to me first."

Sometimes, Sam surprised even herself with her confidence. The way she could talk the talk without worrying if she'd be able to back it up. How her gut settled before big meets. How she could block everything out and focus completely on the race in front of her so that when she dove into that pool, she didn't feel anxious or nervous. She just swam. And won.

"Did you see Keith sulking?" Caroline asked, pointing farther down the row of benches to where the boy sat all by himself.

It had been a few days since the freak accident when his water bottle had exploded in his face, and still no one knew how to explain it. They'd eventually settled on it being a defect, joking that Keith needed to go lighter on the weights, that he didn't know his own strength.

Now he sat on the sidelines wearing sweats and a hoodie. The purple bruising on his chin and cheeks had started to fade to a sallow yellow. But his lips were still swollen and cracked from the impact, which made an odd frame for his brand-new smile. The dentist had outfitted him with a retainer, his fake front teeth shiny and square and obviously not his own. The blockiness of them stood out so much that they kind of made him look like a beaver. Which was probably why he'd stopped smiling. Stopped laughing. Stopped joking altogether. Probably why he was sitting alone while his teammates swam.

"I will never get tired of Keith's buck teeth," Duncan said as he came up behind the girls, doing a poor job of stifling his laughter.

"I actually feel bad for him," Caroline countered, her mouth pouting in sympathy.

"No," Duncan shot right back, his tone becoming more

pointed. "He deserves it. He should feel lucky he only lost his front teeth."

Duncan opened his mouth and stuck out his tongue, a gesture that Keith clearly saw as he retreated farther into his sweatshirt, pulling the hood up to hide his face.

"Be nice." Caroline smacked Duncan with the back of her hand, and he pretended to be hurt by it, rubbing his arm where she'd hit him.

"Not like he's ever been nice to me."

Caroline and Duncan kept up their exchange, volleying back and forth, but Sam wasn't really listening. She was preoccupied, thinking about what had happened to Keith. About that bottle cap. The way the plastic had ballooned and warped under some invisible pressure, a spent artillery shell.

Sam didn't know how it'd happened, but the more she thought about it, the more she realized that she didn't care. She'd been so mad at him in that moment. Had been so fed up with his bullying, his making Duncan into a punch line, a punching bag. She'd wanted something terrible to happen to him. She'd wanted him to hurt. To get some kind of payback for all the mean things he'd done to Duncan. And then he had.

"They're calling for your race," Caroline said, nudging Sam out of her thoughts. "The one hundred is next."

Sam blinked and saw where her friend was pointing toward the blocks.

"Right, time to kick Bailey's butt," she said, rotating her

shoulders and shaking out her arms as she made her way around the pool. She smacked her quads and pulled her cap over her hair. She needed to focus, to get in the zone.

As she came up behind the blocks, her eyes slid to where Bailey stood getting ready. She watched as the girl went through her own prerace routine, spinning her arms in fast windmills, bending over at the edge of the pool, whispering a little prayer or some mantra before splashing a few handfuls of water against her suit. Finishing her ritual, Bailey turned, her gaze narrowing as it met Sam's.

Rivals.

It was clear what Bailey wanted, and Sam was happy to oblige.

Sam tossed her towel onto a chair, then moved to the edge of the pool and dipped her toes in the chilly water. She took a few long, controlled breaths, her chest swelling and contracting with the calming rhythm. She pulled her goggles over her head and pressed the cups into her eye sockets, making microadjustments to the straps until they felt comfortable, until she knew they wouldn't fly off when she dove in.

The one-hundred freestyle was basically an all-out sprint. She needed to capitalize on her underwaters, use her dolphin kick to break through the surface and surge ahead. It was four lengths of the pool. Three turns. Two laps. One winner.

A whistle blew, long and loud and clear, signaling the beginning of the race. Sam stepped up on her block, her arms dangling as she bent over. She could just make out her reflection in the choppy water below, her legs coiled, primed to explode.

As the starter called them to their marks, Sam noticed an odd rippling in the water. A current that distorted her reflection, as if an invisible finger had dragged itself along the surface, pulling her image into something broken and unrecognizable.

It was there and then gone, disappearing before she could identify it. Before she could convince herself of what she'd seen. But it stuck in her mind all the same. Absorbing her. Distracting her so much that, if her instincts hadn't taken over, she would have missed the starter's beep.

Luckily, her body knew what to do. Without even thinking, she flung herself off the block. She leapt headfirst into the race like she'd done so many times before.

When she hit the water, Sam's thoughts peeled away. The only thing that mattered now was the race. Was finishing this one hundred yards as fast as she could.

Counting out her kicks, she broke through the surface, her arms spinning and her feet flying. She threw the water behind her, dumping palmfuls of it in her wake. She got to the first wall and snapped her legs over, catching Bailey in her sights, seeing that she'd already opened up a half-body lead on the girl.

It wasn't enough, though, and Sam kept pushing, jumping off the wall, directing all her momentum in the opposite direction. She surfaced again and barreled through the water, limiting her breathing but keeping tabs on Bailey, watching out of the corner of her eye. She could see the girl hugging the lane line, trying her best to draft off Sam. But she'd need to do more than that if she wanted to keep up. If she wanted to challenge her.

Sam hit the wall and flipped again, entering the second fifty, the back half where races were won and lost. Where she couldn't run on adrenaline alone. She had to concentrate. She had to fight the burn in her lungs and legs and arms. The lactic acid building in her muscles, screaming for her to slow down.

Only, that wasn't her muscles crying out. There was something else ringing in Sam's ears, wailing for her attention. She couldn't stop, though. She had to keep going.

Hitting the final turn, Sam tried to focus. She tried to clear her head. But Bailey was suddenly right there with her. Neck and neck. Sam didn't know how that could have happened. How Bailey could have caught up. But now she only had twenty-five yards left to win this race. She couldn't give up any more ground.

As Sam charged toward the finish, the wailing in her ears became more defined. Became almost impossible to ignore. And suddenly she could distinguish it. She could make out the scream, a girl's, as it echoed through the water every time her head plunged underneath the surface. Her mind was playing tricks on her. Trying to sabotage her. But she wouldn't let it win. She wouldn't let Bailey beat her.

Doing her best to ignore the screams, Sam put her head down and attacked, driving her arms through the water, kicking her legs in thunderous beats. She sprinted home, pouring every ounce of energy she had left into the final length.

And it worked. She was pulling ahead. But then that ripple danced in front of her again. That invisible current slithered her way. It passed over Sam—or did she pass through it?—a pocket of freezing water that took her breath away. That sent chilled needles into her flesh straight down to the bone.

She tried to shake it off, but the cold clung to her. It dragged at her body, tugging her backward. Tugging her down. Panic seized her and she kicked harder. She pulled faster, desperate to reach the wall. To finish. To get out of the water.

The end of the pool came into sight, and Sam gritted her teeth, adding her own scream to the water as she pushed home and punched her hand into the wall.

Immediately, she yanked her goggles off, holding tight to the lip of the pool. She looked over and saw Bailey there at the wall with her, looking just as tired but also triumphant. A different kind of panic rose in Sam, and her eyes flew to the scoreboard. Had she lost? To Bailey?

Relief spilled over her when she saw the first place next to her name. But she'd only won by a tenth of a second. Not even the blink of an eye. It was too close. It gave Bailey an opening. Hope.

Sam's gaze slid back to Bailey, to the smug look on her

face, and then to the pool, to that unseen thing lurking in its depths. Her pulse quivered in her neck, too fast to count the beats. Too fast to be from the race alone. Without a word, Sam pulled herself out of the pool, forgetting her towel in her haste to get away.

"Hey," someone called to her, but Sam wasn't listening. She couldn't concentrate. "Hey, I was going to congratulate you—"

Caroline faltered as she came up to Sam, as she saw the look of terror on her face.

"Wait. What happened? What's the matter?"

For a split second, Sam thought about telling her friend the truth. About acknowledging that creeping cold that had stolen over her at the end of the race, that had tried to stop her in the water, to pull her under. But how unhinged would she sound? So instead, she tried to harness that confidence she always had in the pool. That strength. She tried to ignore the scream, the eerie shriek that was still playing in her ears.

"I'm fine," she said, plastering on a smile. "Everything's fine. I won."

But even as she said it, her eyes strayed to the pool. She strained to see that ripple, that invisible current. She racked her brain trying to figure out what it could have been.

CHAPTER
ELEVEN

The pool had emptied out by the time Sam coasted into the wall and finished up her cooldown. Removing her goggles and shaking her ears dry, she lifted herself onto the wall and took a seat. She let her feet dangle out in front of her, watching the currents make their patterns in the water. She hadn't forgotten the chilly feeling that had engulfed her when she'd been racing Bailey, but time had blurred its edges. Had made Sam think that maybe she'd overreacted or imagined it. After all, the pool got cold pockets of water like that all the time. And she'd been in the middle of a race, her pulse pounding, her adrenaline pumping, her brain and muscles screaming for oxygen. She couldn't be sure of what she'd heard. Of what she'd thought she'd felt.

Sam exhaled and closed her eyes. She let the lapping of the water wash over her. The familiar rhythm lulled her into a peaceful place. It soothed her and reminded her of why she swam, why she felt so at home in the pool. When it was just her and the water, she was in control. She was safe.

Just then, Sam's body pitched forward.

She only managed to stay out of the pool by the sheer force of her fingers gripping the edge, turning white as they lost circulation from the strain. She pulled herself up and scrambled back, ripping her feet from the water, thinking that one of the currents had grabbed her, had tried to drag her in. But then she heard laughter behind her and realized who the real culprit was.

"Drowning me?" Sam asked as she flipped around, hoping that her question came out with every ounce of acid she was feeling. "Is that really how you plan to beat me? But then, I guess it's the only way you could."

Bailey's smirk disappeared and turned into a scowl. Her jaw clenched and she looked ready to throw a punch. But she restrained herself. She collected herself and rearranged her face, painting on a too-sweet smile. "I wanted to congratulate you on a great race. On your win."

"Thanks," Sam said wearily. She didn't know where Bailey was going with this, but she nodded along, hoping she could get it over with fast. "You swam really well, too. You were right there with me. Less than a second behind."

"A tenth of a second," Bailey corrected her, with a tone crisp and precise, leaving no room for error.

"Like I said, less than a second."

And then Sam shrugged, delighting in the nonchalance of it, in the way Bailey reacted, the vein in her temple throbbing, pulsing with rage.

"I'm coming for you," Bailey huffed, her emotions spilling over. "I'm close and getting closer. I won't lose again. I promise you that."

And then, as if her words weren't enough of a threat, Bailey leaned down and snatched Sam's water bottle off the deck.

"Hey!" Sam leapt to her feet and went charging after Bailey. But she was too late. Her nemesis had already managed to grab what she wanted, to pry Sam's necklace away from the water bottle.

"Not so tough without your lucky charms," Bailey taunted.

"Give that back!"

But Bailey didn't listen. She held Sam's necklace just out of reach, letting it dangle there, the seashell and laurel wreath swinging this way and that in time to some sick version of eenie, meenie, miney, mo.

"If you want them so bad, then you can go get them." And without warning, Bailey drew her arm back and launched Sam's necklace. It soared out over the pool, glittering in the light, sailing and then plummeting as it plopped into the water and sank beneath the surface.

"You—" Sam couldn't believe it. But she didn't have time to rant or fight. She had to go in after her necklace. She didn't have that much time to search if she wanted to make it to her first class on time. So, without wasting another word on Bailey, Sam pressed her goggles into her face and dove back into the pool.

The water met her with its cool embrace, rushing into her ears to say hello, to drown out the laughter Bailey was surely enjoying at Sam's expense. To hell with her, though, and her sour grapes. She better get used to coming in second, because Sam wasn't going to go easy on her. She wasn't going to let up. If anything, she was more motivated now. She'd crush Bailey and not feel a bit bad about doing it.

Swimming through the water, Sam made for the deep end, where she'd seen her necklace go under. She kept telling herself that she'd find it. That it wasn't lost. It was the only thing she had left of Kasey, a last reminder of the friend she'd lost. It couldn't be replaced.

She took a deep breath and then dove under, the water pressure building as she descended, the static turning into a whistle until she popped her ears and recalibrated, her feet touching the bottom, anchoring her twelve feet below the surface. Her head swiveled as she swept the area, straining to catch every minute detail. The world around her had taken on an eerie gray tint, the shade of her goggles coloring everything in sepia tones.

Pushing off, Sam widened her search, her palms skimming the bottom of the pool, rubbing against fine bits of sand

and dirt and ground-up fiberglass. She was looking for anything shiny, anything that did not belong.

A darting movement out of the corner of her eye caught her attention, and she followed it. She drifted to the corner of the deep end, her eyes open, watchful. And then she spotted it, a glimmer in the water: her necklace. A bubble popped out of her mouth as she grew excited, as she pushed to retrieve the keepsake. But as she closed in on it, a strange feeling crept over her. The hairs on her arm prickled as the shrill whistle of water pressure blew back into her ears. Her lungs squeezed and she realized she'd been under for longer than she'd thought. She was approaching her limit. But the necklace was right there. She'd grab it and be back on the surface in seconds.

Reaching out, Sam's fingers pressed into another pocket of ice-cold water. She shivered but kept going. The chilliness climbed up her arms, clung to her shoulders, wrapped all the way around her until she was encased in it. The water pressure built to a roar in her ears. It shrieked with a deafening insistence. But Sam was so close. Her fingers grazed the necklace. She had it in her palm. She made to push off, to rocket to the surface, but something kept her down, kept her from escaping. It was almost like a hand had reached out and clamped down on her shoulder.

Turning, Sam fully expected there to be someone floating behind her. But it was only empty water, a cold void.

Another breath pushed out of Sam's lungs as she gasped, as

the whistling in her ears changed into something recognizable. Into her own name.

Sam.

Her eyebrows furrowed as she looked all around, as she tried to find a body for that voice. But she was alone. All by herself.

Sam.

The voice pierced through her head again.

Don't forget me.

Sam startled, her heart suddenly in her throat. Her necklace pulsed in her palm, and she unclasped her fingers to look at it, to examine the tiny seashell charm.

Was it Kasey? Was she trying to speak to Sam? After all these years?

Don't let them silence you the way they silenced me.

No. That couldn't be Kasey. It had to be—

Sam gulped at the thought, as realization crashed into her and it became clear.

The other charm warmed in her hand. It seemed to glow. With her thumb, she pressed down on it. The laurel leaves bit into her flesh, a sharp pain that revealed a vision of the past, of a lonely girl. Of Missy.

Sam recognized her immediately. She was much younger than she'd been in the photos Sam had found online, maybe eight years old, but her tight, curly hair was unmistakable, was so full that Sam wondered how she fit it all underneath her swim cap.

This child version of Missy stood on the edge of a pool in

the middle of summer, the sun beating down on her shoulders. Sam thought it was the graveyard pool, but it was hard to tell. It looked so different filled, the clear blue water brimming to the top, spilling over.

"Incoming!"

The shout came out of nowhere. And then blue and red and green missiles burst against the pool deck, the water balloons popping with sharp snaps. Missy squealed as one hit her in the head. She ducked down as another exploded against her stomach. In two seconds she was soaked, but the onslaught continued, the boys wielding their toy grenades coming into sight, moving in for the kill. Missy was surrounded, so she did the only thing she could. She jumped into the pool, retreating from the fight.

The boys on the deck burst into laughter, pointing at Missy, making fun of the way she cowered in the water, her arms still up to protect against another attack.

A girl came up to them then, and Sam sucked in a breath. She looked just like Bailey. But that was impossible. Bailey would have barely been born. But, Sam thought, her sister would have been the exact right age.

Sam watched as the girl talked to the boys, as she seemed to be negotiating with them, maybe even chastising them. She held her hand out and one of the boys put his water balloon in it. Then she turned to the pool, called to Missy like it was safe for her to come out.

Letting her guard down, a relieved smile flitted onto Missy's face. But it was wiped away just as quickly as Bailey's sister cocked her arm and threw the water balloon right at her.

The missile exploded against Missy's chest, and she let out a pathetic yelp, one that was quickly eaten up by the barking laughter of the boys and Bailey's sister. And all Sam could do as she watched Missy sink below the surface, the water rushing over her head and drowning out the ridicule, was feel terrible for her.

Sam's lungs burned as she came back to the present. Remembering where she was, she pushed off the bottom of the pool and came bursting through the surface, her mouth open, taking gasping breaths of sweet oxygen. She coughed and paddled to a nearby ladder. She climbed out of the pool and collapsed on the deck. After a few minutes, she got up and grabbed her towel. She wrapped it around her shoulders, but even so, the cold stayed with her. It froze her bones and made goose bumps of her flesh. It made her realize that what she'd seen down there and what she'd felt in her race against Bailey, that the wet footprints she'd found in her hallway the night before and the bathtub overflowing with bloody water . . . it was real. Her imagination couldn't have made that all up. And there was no way Bailey could pull off such an elaborate prank.

It was real. It was Missy.

CHAPTER
TWELVE

"Did we really have to come out here in the middle of the night?" Duncan whispered, shining his flashlight ahead of them as they picked their way across the grass field.

"It works best when there's a full moon," Caroline explained, her excitement the exact opposite of Sam's dread.

"Which isn't tonight," Duncan noted.

"No, but it's close enough," Caroline replied, skipping ahead, leaving Sam to pause and look up at the waning gibbous overhead, the sickle of light hanging like a blade in the sky. A bad omen.

Sam shivered as she remembered what she'd experienced underwater, that glimpse into Missy's past, the girl's voice in her head, the sharp cold of death enveloping her. She hadn't wanted to believe it, but how else could she explain it? Missy was trying to speak to her. And Sam needed to figure out why. She had to face this, no matter how much it scared her. She couldn't let anything get in the way of her training. She couldn't let anything keep her out of the pool.

Thankfully, she didn't have to do this alone. She'd been kind of surprised when her friends had both jumped at the chance to help. But perhaps she should have known how well acquainted her fellow swimmers would have been with superstitions. They would do anything it took to help Sam overcome what she needed to in order to stay ahead of Bailey. Caroline even seemed to know a thing or two about communing with the dead. At least, she'd had an old Ouija board stowed away in her closet, one that she'd toyed around with at a few middle school slumber parties. She knew the ritual, knew what they needed to do to invite Missy's spirit to visit them. Now Sam just had to hope that it worked. That Missy would appear. That they could figure out what she wanted and how to make her go away.

"Come on," Caroline called over her shoulder.

Sam adjusted her backpack and hurried to catch up. She didn't think Caroline completely believed her story. But then, who would? It was all a little out there. A little bit spooky and far-fetched. Ghosts didn't exist. At least, Sam hadn't thought they did until a day ago.

"We're here." Caroline gestured excitedly at the chain-link fence in front of them, the hole that Bailey had led them through on a night not too long ago.

Before Sam could think better of it, she ducked under, holding her breath until she came out on the other side. She waited as Duncan and Caroline shuffled through after her; then they were inside, the abandoned Wentworth Public Pool looming like an empty grave in front of them.

"It didn't seem this creepy last time," Duncan said as he swept his flashlight beam across the pool, spotlighting the dirt and decay, the graffiti and skateboard tracks. The diving board lay flat in the middle of the deep end, a detail Sam hadn't noticed before. She'd thought the city had come in and removed it for safety reasons, but it looked like they'd left it out to weather and rot like everything else, to crack and disintegrate until there was nothing left holding it together.

"Let's go," Caroline said, her voice pushing them forward, keeping them on task.

Sam nodded and the three of them made their way to the shallow end, climbing down the same rusted ladder that left them standing in the pool, the warped plastic lining buckling under their feet.

"I'm guessing she drowned in the deep end." Sam kept moving, trying her best not to hesitate. She didn't want to waste a second. Because if she stalled, she didn't know if she'd be able to go through with it. This ritual. This communion with the dead.

As they descended the pool's slope, moving farther underground with each step, the walls rose up and towered above them. Sam craned her neck and took it all in, reading the graffiti, the names and epitaphs spray-painted there—JASON WAS HERE, YOU ONLY LIVE ONCE, TELL MY MOTHER I LOVE HER. They were words to be remembered by, to have memorialized on a tombstone.

"Is this good?"

Sam jerked her head around as Caroline pointed at the downed diving board. "Yeah. That should work."

Sam swung her bag around and set it on the ground, kneeling as she rummaged through it. Hands shaking, she pulled out candles and a matchbook. She unearthed a canister of salt and a small bowl. She took out her water bottle and then the Ouija board Caroline had given her.

"This is everything we need, right?" Sam asked, waiting for Caroline to take inventory. After a couple of seconds, the girl nodded. She bit her lower lip and got to work, laying everything out on the diving board, using the piece of fiberglass like a makeshift altar.

First, she opened the salt canister and carefully traced a wide circle around the board, big enough for them all to fit inside.

"This is supposed to protect us," she whispered. "In case things get out of hand."

Sam gulped, hoping that wouldn't be the case.

"And this is how we'll summon Missy's spirit." Caroline placed the empty bowl next to the Ouija board she'd laid out on the diving board and grabbed Sam's water bottle. She squirted a stream into the basin of the dish, careful not to spill any of it. "You got it from the school pool, right?"

Sam quickly nodded.

"Good. I figured the chlorinated water would remind Missy of this place. Help us call her back."

Neither Duncan nor Sam had anything to say about that, so Caroline kept going, finishing with her setup and then handing each of them a candle.

"Now, there's only one last thing . . ."

Caroline reached into her pocket and pulled out a thin sewing needle. She held it high so Duncan and Sam could see its slender shaft catching in the flashlight's beam, glittering and dangerous.

"Give me your hand," Caroline said to Sam. "Since she's haunting you, it's got to be your blood."

With a little bit of hesitation, Sam offered up her palm. And then, without much fanfare, Caroline plunged the tip of the needle into her finger. Sam gasped at the bright pain and the dot of blood that bubbled up to meet it. She watched as the liquid ballooned, transfixed by the crimson color, by how much darker and richer it looked coming out of her now, in the middle of the night, in a forsaken place like this. The bead of blood swelled in size, holding on to its spherical shape until it threatened to burst. Only then did Caroline guide her hand over, turning Sam's palm so that the blood dribbled into the bowl of water, swirling and then slowly combining into one mixture.

"Okay. Now we light the candles." Caroline picked up the matchbook. "And turn off the flashlight."

Sam gulped as Caroline's eyes met hers. As Duncan gave her an are-you-sure-about-this look. The pool was so much scarier in the dark. But it had to be done. The ceremony wouldn't work otherwise. And so, Sam nodded.

With the click of a button, the light flickered out and they were plunged into gloom. The sickle moon provided some relief, but it couldn't combat the dark, the shifting shadows that seemed to amplify the nighttime noises around them, owls hooting and crickets chirping. The scuttling of feet—mice or lizards or maybe something worse.

Sam's skin crawled, but she didn't bolt. She didn't scream out. She closed her eyes and took a moment, then she reached out and Caroline handed her the matches. She struck one, the flame sizzling to life, blooming and then spreading as she lit all three of their candles. She bent over and set hers on the diving board altar, Caroline and Duncan following suit. Then she sat down, the three of them forming a circle around the Ouija board and the bowl.

"What now?" Duncan asked, fidgeting as his eyes darted every which way.

"Now we call her spirit to us," Caroline said in a shockingly solemn tone. "Everyone, put your fingers on the planchette. And Sam, it's your turn with the invocation."

Sam's palms were slick as the three of them reached forward, anchoring themselves to the Ouija board. She inhaled, wisps of smoke tickling her throat, and blew the breath back out. Then, following along with the script Caroline had given her on the drive over, she started to speak, aiming her voice up into the night.

"Missy Caplin, we respectfully ask you to join us here tonight."

She tried to remember all the words that Caroline had scribbled down. But then she remembered that her friend had also warned her that it wasn't just what she said, but also her intention. Her belief that Missy's spirit was out there. That she would answer the call. The drowned girl's ghost would only respond if Sam willed it.

"Missy Caplin," Sam tried again, flashing back to the bottom of the pool, to the memory that had overtaken her, remembering the grip it'd held on her, the corporeality of it. "Please, hear us. Join our circle. Let us know you're here."

She repeated the line, pressing down on the planchette as her friends took up the call, chanting the words over and over again, together, their invitation unspooling from their mouths, wrapping around them, adding to the night's noises, to nature's hum of life and death. Sam closed her eyes and surrendered to the darkness. She let it envelop her. Their voices continued to swim around her, but then they started to fade, to get lost in the background. And suddenly, Sam was somewhere else entirely, floating all alone in a vast sea. Shipwrecked and adrift.

Waves rocked her from side to side, so hard that she had to hold on tight to the raft beneath her. A distant moaning filled her ears, coming from everywhere and nowhere at the same time. Inching forward, she hazarded a glance overboard, spotting her reflection outlined there in the black mirror of the water.

At first, she looked like herself. But then, as she stared at her image longer, she started to change. Her hair grew thin and patchy. Her cheeks hollowed out to nothing. Her skin lost its shine, turning pale and prune-like, peeling off in places so that her bones started to peek through.

She raised her hands to touch her face, to make sure she was still there, but her fingers had swelled, had puckered and creased, had become so bloated with water that she couldn't feel a thing. She dropped them, disgusted and afraid, her body trembling as a new horror gripped her, as she glanced back down into the water and saw a demon staring up at her. Only it wasn't her own warped reflection anymore. It was Missy. Or what was left of her. Their eyes met for a second, a curiosity passing between them. An understanding. Then Missy's arms launched through the surface. She grabbed Sam by the shoulders and yanked her overboard, dragging her under.

Sam gasped as she came up for air. As the wind shifted,

turning cool and sharp and whipping. Her eyes snapped open in time to see the candles sputter, their flames leaping and dancing, threatening to go out. Her blood swirled in the bowl next to the Ouija board, separating from the water, spiraling into a whirlpool that looked like it wanted to suck them all under. The planchette tugged underneath her fingertips, pulling her this way and that, spelling out a message too fast for Sam to comprehend.

A howl wound through the night, and Sam felt Missy's presence with them, the girl's spirit swimming around their protective salt circle, gasping and spitting, in search of water, something it could submerge itself in. It carried a frantic energy, an unquenchable anger. But Sam also sensed a profound sadness there. A life cut short. An emptiness that could never be filled.

Sam was slipping. Her fingers were starting to peel away from the planchette, from her connection to Duncan and Caroline. But they pressed in next to her. They refused to let go. And in that, they grounded her. They brought her back from the edge.

"We see you, Missy," Sam shouted, struggling to be heard over the gusts of wind. "And we ask you, what do you want? What do you need so that you can cross over to the other side?"

Sam strained to make out the message on the board. But Missy wasn't spelling anything. It was only random letters, an overload. Instead, the spirit's wail grew louder. It turned into a screech. But Sam kept going, willing strength into her voice, imagining she was on the final lap of a distance race, pushing through the pain and fear, sprinting for the finish line.

"Please. Tell us. Let us help you."

But again, the spirit didn't listen. It didn't answer. It only grew more agitated. The wind picked up. It battered them from all sides, began to shift the salt crystals, threatened to break their circle wide open, to fling them into harm's way.

"What do you want from me?" Sam screamed, trying one last time to get through, her throat raw as she emptied every bit of energy she had into the command. "Tell me. Please."

She was desperate now, but as the wind picked up and the roar swelled in her ears, Sam knew her time was up. Missy was too angry. Too unstable to listen to her. Sam wouldn't get the answers she needed. Not without putting them all in danger.

"Leave us alone," Sam cried out. "Go! Now!"

But Missy's presence continued to swirl around them. It closed in, snatching at Sam's short hair, scratching at her arms, trying to pry her away from her friends, to drag her back into that dark netherworld.

"Goodbye!"

At the last second, Caroline's voice cut through the night. And with a piercing shriek that echoed off the pool walls, Missy disappeared. Everything grew suddenly still. Caroline leapt forward and doused the candles in the bowl of water, throwing them all into complete darkness. A few seconds later, the flashlight snapped on, the beam aimed directly at Sam's face, wobbling in Duncan's shaky hand.

"Did that really just happen?" he asked.

Slowly, Sam nodded. She could still feel where Missy's claws had sunk into her flesh and was sure there would be cuts and bruises tomorrow to prove that it had all been very real.

"Is it over?"

"It should be." This time it was Caroline who answered Duncan's question. "We closed the door. We said goodbye."

"But does that mean she's gone for good?" Sam had to ask the question, even though she didn't want to hear the answer. Even though she knew in her gut what it would be.

"I—" Caroline paused, still caught up in the moment, in what had happened, in how impossible it all seemed. But then, hadn't she experienced it? Hadn't she seen and heard and felt it all just now? "I don't think so."

And Sam could only agree. She could only gulp down her fear, swallow her misgivings. Because this haunting—or whatever she wanted to call it—wasn't over yet.

CHAPTER
THIRTEEN

Sam had barely gotten through the last week of practice. Every time she got into the pool she nearly had a panic attack. The anxiety was killing her. The fear had her almost stopping at every single wall. It was so much worse now because Sam knew that Missy was down there, lurking, waiting for her to drop her guard. She was nipping at Sam's toes, her moans echoing through the water like an ominous whale song, her freezing presence floating through the lanes, following in Sam's wake. Whenever Sam felt that chilly pocket come upon her, she'd keep her head down and close her eyes. She'd swim through it with her breath held tight, her arms poised to fly or to grab on to a lane line if she felt even the pinch of a tug.

Staring out at the water, Sam's eyes darted this way and that, searching as she thought back to a week ago, when she and Duncan and Caroline had climbed down into the abandoned Wentworth Public Pool and called upon Missy's spirit. She hadn't gotten answers then, and she'd been too afraid to try again. The way that Missy had howled and clawed and nearly pulled her into that empty, in-between place . . . it still sent chills through her body. It kept her up at night. And it was even starting to affect her swimming.

She pushed through because it was her only option. She had to get her laps in. She had to keep moving. She couldn't let up for anything. She couldn't afford to fall behind Bailey. She couldn't risk disappointing her dad.

"I thought we were going to play a game." Bailey's bored voice interrupted Sam's thoughts, bringing her back to the moment. She could hear the other girls snickering behind her back, their captain eating up the attention she was getting from her audience.

"I thought it was time to go home," Sam countered, already over Bailey. They'd just finished up a team dinner. The parents had brought pots and casserole dishes full of warm pasta to the high school pool for them to eat in preparation for their first official meet the following night. Now Sam was full and exhausted, carbo-loaded to the max. She just wanted to get out of there. Get as far away from Bailey and the water as she could.

"But I'm not tired yet," Bailey said, pouting her lips and stomping her foot like a brat.

Sam's expression soured and she had to fight the urge to yawn right in the girl's face. It wouldn't do her any favors to challenge Bailey now. The girl had the whole team on her side. Either they were afraid to step out of line or they were desperately trying to gain her approval by acquiescing to her jokes and nodding along to every cruelty she could come up with. So instead, Sam gritted her teeth and asked, "What did you have in mind?"

"Truth or dare." Bailey didn't hesitate as a saccharine-sweet smile spread across her face.

Sam rolled her eyes. Of course. She wished she'd bummed a ride home with her dad earlier when the dinner had broken up. But now she had no excuse. She had to play along or endure Bailey's wrath. Her ridicule if she chickened out.

"I'll go first," Bailey chirped, her gaze darting around the circle of girls, sizing up her victims. "Paige. Truth or dare?"

The freshman girl jumped, and Sam couldn't decide if she was excited to be called on first, to confirm that Bailey knew her name, knew of her existence, or if she was terrified of what the senior had in mind for her.

"Truth," she whispered, her expression screwed up into a grimace as she waited.

Bailey took her time thinking it over, tilting her head this way and that as if she was in deep thought. Then she leaned forward and opened her mouth. "Is it true that you've never kissed a boy?"

Paige blanched at the question, her grimace turning into a frown. She ducked her head as everyone turned to her, as they waited for the juicy answer. And then, slowly, hesitantly, she nodded. Bailey broke out into an immediate fit of giggles, which the rest of the girls quickly parroted, and Paige seemed to shrink even more.

Sam felt bad for her. She knew what it was like to be the butt of one of Bailey's jokes. And even though Paige had sucked up to Bailey multiple times, had come for Sam in the locker room and spread lies about her, it made Sam furious. She didn't think anyone deserved to be treated this cruelly.

"Your turn, Bailey," Sam jumped in, not giving anyone else a chance to speak. "Truth or dare?"

Bailey waited a beat, locked in a staring contest with Sam, and then she spoke. "Dare."

The girls all oohed as Bailey rose to Sam's challenge, and Sam had to scramble to think of something that would be good enough. That would put Bailey in her place.

"I dare you to—" Sam broke off as she looked around. "I dare you to drink out of the pool. Like you were a dog."

A flutter of excitement bubbled up in Sam's stomach as she watched Bailey's lip curl. Swallowing a little pool water never hurt anyone. They'd all done it in practice. But having to lap it up like a dog . . . Sam hoped someone had their phone out. She wanted to watch this back on repeat.

"Easy." Bailey smirked, recovering quickly from her earlier distaste. And as if she needed to prove her nonchalance, she sauntered toward the edge of the pool, luxuriating in the spotlight, putting on a show. She took her time getting down on her knees, and then, making sure that everyone was watching, she stuck out her tongue and licked the water. Four. Five. And then six times. Finishing, she got up and wiped her chin. She walked back to the group and took a bow, everyone applauding her performance as not a single girl laughed.

"You ready for your dare?" Bailey sounded so wicked as she turned the tables around on Sam. But now Sam had to go through with it. She couldn't back down.

"Fine," Sam said, the answer coming out harsh. Coming out angry. She was sick of Bailey and how she kept toying with her. Sam would never get to make the rules, but if she played by Bailey's and won, then maybe the girl would finally leave her alone.

"I dare you to . . ." Bailey paused as she thought it over, no doubt trying to come up with the worst thing possible. "I dare you to go for a swim. Right now. In your underwear."

Her lips smacked with the challenge, a kiss of death. And Sam wondered if she somehow knew how afraid Sam was of the water. Of what was beneath the surface.

"She doesn't need to prove anything to you," Caroline announced, stepping up beside Sam. But Sam only patted her friend's arm, signaling for her to back down. As much as she hated it, Sam had to do this. She couldn't let Bailey win again.

"I've got this," Sam said.

Bailey's smile faltered, but only for a second. She was still in charge. Still in control. "Let's see it, then," she purred, her arms crossed and her hip cocked in defiance.

Sam nodded and turned to the pool. When she was sure that no one could see her face, she bit her bottom lip and gulped. She stood there and stared out into the water, straining to catch any ripple of movement.

"Are you there, Missy?" she whispered, even though she didn't expect to get a response. "Please, just leave me alone. Let me get through this." She closed her eyes as if sending up a prayer, and then she slipped her shoes off. And her dress, so that she stood there in only her bra and underwear. She snuck a glance over her shoulder and saw everyone staring at her, waiting for her plunge. It was now or never. No going back.

Sam took a deep breath and dipped her toe in. She shivered. But was it actually freezing? Or was Sam's body playing tricks on her? She could feel everyone's eyes pinned to her back, but she didn't turn to look at them. She kept her focus on the pool. On the water. On any movement in it. She had to be brave. She had to get through this.

Not allowing herself the time to give it any more thought, Sam knelt and slid in, breaking the seal in one movement. Her hand still gripped the wall tight. It helped her keep her head above the surface, but also, something in her gut told her to hold on, to remain anchored to solid ground.

"That doesn't count," Bailey piped up, tsking and shaking her head like Sam had cheated or broken an unspoken rule.

"You've got to swim out to the middle of the deep end."

Sam hesitated. Her fingers refused to bend. Refused to let go. But she had to do this. So, knuckle by knuckle, Sam forced her grip to lift. To release its hold. She came loose from the wall and floated there in the water on her own. She took a few breaststrokes and moved away from everyone else, gliding silently out into the center of the pool, her arms and legs on high alert, sensing for the faintest tremor, for the first sign that she needed to get out of there. When she reached the middle, she stopped. She kicked her legs and sculled with her hands to tread water.

"This good enough for you?" she asked defiantly, throwing it in Bailey's face, showing her up.

"I guess you win," Bailey called back. But there was something wrong with the way the girl said it. The beatific smile on her face didn't match that of someone who had just lost. And a second later, Sam realized why. "Hope you brought extra clothes."

On Bailey's command, Paige swept her leg forward and kicked Sam's dress into the water.

"You can't—" Sam protested, not understanding what had just happened. She glowered at Paige, who Bailey must have put up to the prank. But why would the freshman go along with it? Bailey had humiliated her not more than a minute ago. Did she really want her captain's approval that badly? Did she have no dignity?

Rage stirred in Sam's stomach. It radiated off her, practically boiling the water in the pool. But no one seemed to notice. No one cared to move or sympathize, not while Bailey laughed, while they all joined in.

At the edge of the pool, Paige flitted about, skipping back and forth, delighted in the part she'd played in the prank. She was trying to get Bailey's attention with her over-the-top giggles. With her pointing out of Sam's clothes, of how they'd already started to sink to the bottom. But when that didn't work, Paige turned her attention on Sam. She took out her phone and started snapping photos, bending and crouching to get Sam from every angle, to get as close as possible.

"This is great," Paige said, painfully earnest in her attempts to make Bailey notice her. It was so bad that even Bailey didn't acknowledge it. Didn't acknowledge the girl at all, until Paige's foot slipped, until she lost her balance and tumbled headfirst and fully clothed into the pool.

Silence fell in the wake of her splash. But as soon as Paige's drenched head came bobbing up to break the surface, a fit of laughter exploded, ten times louder than what Sam had endured. Bailey convulsed with glee, pointing and shaking, wringing every last drop of humiliation out of Paige. They didn't say it, but Sam knew what they were all thinking. And, judging by the way Paige's head sagged, so did she.

Loser.

Sam knew the weight of that word, but she didn't care. Not

after what Paige had done. Sam was furious. Would have pulled Paige in herself if she'd had the chance. Getting soaked. Getting laughed at. It was what she deserved.

"That's too good," Bailey sighed from the deck, wiping the tears from her eyes as a cluster of hiccups bubbled out of her.

Then, without offering to help either girl out of the pool, Bailey turned and sauntered away, the rest of the team following in her wake, their laughter an echo that grew quieter until the girls had all disappeared.

"You know you deserved that, right?" Sam said, taking a few strokes and coming closer to Paige. Fury coursed through her, but on some level, she knew that Paige wasn't to blame. That the girl had only taken part in Bailey's plan and not come up with it on her own. But a pawn was a pawn. And Sam could still hold Paige accountable for her actions.

"Why do you go along with her? Why do you cater to every sadistic thought that pops into her head? You're only making it worse. For me. And for yourself."

Paige didn't say anything. She only gave Sam a cold shoulder, sniffling as she turned away, as she refused to acknowledge anything Sam had said. Her hair was plastered against her forehead in a disheveled mess, and it looked like her phone had sunk to the bottom of the pool. But still, there was no remorse. No apology.

"Oh my gosh, are you okay?" Sam's attention snapped up to the deck, where Caroline was kneeling, attempting to fish Sam's dress out of the water. "I'm sorry. I should have stepped in sooner. I should have stopped her before—but I didn't know what she was going to do. I thought you'd beaten her."

"It's okay," Sam said, taking one last glance at Paige's back before she gave up on getting through to her. "I needed to handle that on my own. I can't have you fighting all my battles."

"Let's get you dry and we can figure out something for you to wear."

Sam nodded and made for the edge of the pool. But just as she started her stroke, something shifted in the water. A cold swell washed over her toes and goose bumps ran up her arms. She could sense Missy below, circling like a shark, ready to attack. Her eyes darted this way and that, trying to spot Missy's spirit, straining to see the disturbance. But there was nothing but clear water all around her. Nothing in sight.

The pool rippled again and Sam flinched. Her heart stopped. Her lungs constricted. Her body sagged and she sank low in the water, her senses on high alert, her fingers outstretched, feeling out the subtle shifts, the lapping currents, tracking with her own kind of sonar.

"Paige," she said quietly, intensely. "We need to get out of the water *now*."

As she spoke, she tried to calculate the distance, the time it'd take to get to the wall. If they sprinted, it'd only take seconds. But was that enough time to escape?

"On the count of three, we make a break for the wall. As fast as you can go."

"What?" Paige blubbered.

"Just do it."

And Sam hoped that was enough. That Paige would listen. Would save herself.

"One. Two." Sam inhaled a deep breath, her muscles tightening. "Three."

And she took off, kicking toward the wall, toward dry land and safety. Her legs churned behind her as her arms whipped around. She could feel Missy notice, could feel her take off, shooting through the water like a torpedo after them. But they were going to make it, the edge of the pool was almost in reach.

Sam got there first, her palm smacking the solid lip of the pool, an anchor for her to hang on to. Paige was a few strokes behind, slowed down by her shoes and wet clothes. Sam stretched her arm out toward the girl, their fingers touching, connecting. But then they slid apart. Sam clocked the moment that Paige recognized something was wrong, a look of confusion and pain contorting her features, blowing out in a yelp as something yanked her under, as her head disappeared beneath the pool's surface.

"No!" Sam shouted, letting go of the wall and diving after Paige.

She followed the trail of bubbles, swimming down to meet the submerged girl, to help pull her free. Their hands collided and Sam tugged, straining as she kicked toward the surface, as Paige dragged her deeper. Paige's eyes bulged, her mouth open in an unheard scream. Terror transformed her face, made it unbearable for Sam to take in. But when she looked past Paige, her eyes stinging from the chlorine, she saw her. She saw Missy. Only this time she wasn't viewing it from behind closed eyes. This wasn't a nightmare or her imagination. This was real. Inches from her face. The thing that had been terrifying her for weeks. A ghost before her eyes.

Even though time and the water had warped her appearance—bloated her flesh so that it pulled away from her bones, floating there on its own, shifting and distorted and disturbing like a bulbous rubber mask—Sam recognized Missy from the pictures she'd found online and from the tattered suit that she wore, the Wentworth High School *W* emblazoned on the chest.

Sam pulled back, a gasp robbing her of her last breath. Her grip on Paige loosened, came undone. She pushed to the surface, her lungs aching for oxygen, screaming to get away. Air rushed down her throat, filling her up. But she couldn't rest. She couldn't—

"Get out of there," Caroline cried from the side of the pool.

"I have to help her." Sam floundered over the words.

"It's too late," Caroline shouted back, her hand flying to grab Sam's wrist, to yank her out of the pool. Out of danger. "There's nothing you can do."

"I can't leave her down there."

As Sam tried to rip her arm free of Caroline's grip, pain

suddenly lanced through her ankle, needles burying themselves into her flesh. She cried out and then screamed as the demon reeled her in.

"Sam!"

Caroline's hand slipped as she held on, as she balanced her weight and tried to keep Sam from drowning. She strained and tugged, and Sam thought her shoulder might pop out of its socket. But then, with an excruciating effort, Sam came loose. She flopped onto the deck and scrambled away from the water, her heart pounding wildly in her chest, her hands shaking as she watched the pool, as she took in the five trails of blood streaming down her leg where Missy's claws had left their mark. A gasp died in the back of her throat and her eyes went big and round and struck with horror as a body came bobbing up to the surface.

Paige floated there, facedown and unmoving, her hair fanned out around her. Sam blinked and shook her head. She had to be seeing things. This couldn't be real. Paige couldn't be . . .

A scream echoed through the pool, and Sam looked up to see Bailey standing there on the other side of the deep end. She screamed again and Coach Hendricks came spilling out of his office, his expression confused and then stunned by what he saw. By the drowned girl floating lifelessly in the middle of the high school pool.

CHAPTER
FOURTEEN

Sam, Caroline, and Bailey sat across from Coach Hendricks, their chairs creaking as they rocked back and forth, every single one of them stunned. They waited in the prickly quiet that had fallen after all the screaming had died down. After someone—and Sam honestly couldn't remember who—had pulled Paige's body out of the pool. After they'd laid it out on the deck. After they'd covered it with a towel so that no one had to look at her pale, lifeless face.

Paige was dead. It didn't make sense, but it was the truth. It seemed like it had happened days ago, but no more than ten minutes could have passed. It had been a blur. A hurricane of splashing water and gasping breaths. Of flailing limbs and straining muscles. Of fear and desperation. And now it was all over. They couldn't change what had happened. They couldn't bring Paige back. They were just waiting for the paramedics to arrive. For the police to come and question them. There'd be an accident report. A cause of death. A story that would need to tie it all together, to make sense of the unspeakable thing that had happened.

"So," Coach Hendricks began, breaking the silence as delicately as he could, like dipping a toe in the water. "Can you tell me what happened out there?"

His voice sounded calm—too calm—a soothing tone that belied the way his fidgeting fingertips drummed against the desk, never slowing, never ceasing, pounding out their own nervous rhythm.

"I know you must be in shock," he went on. "But I can help. I can talk to the police if you'll open up to me. What happened after dinner? How did Paige end up in the pool? How did she drown?"

Sam shifted in her seat. She pulled the towel she'd been given tighter against her shoulders. A shiver ran through her even though she was curled in a ball, her knees pressed against her chest, her arms hugging them close. She didn't know what to say or how to say it. She knew what she'd seen. But she didn't know how she could explain it to Coach Hendricks so that he'd believe her.

"It was an accident," Bailey said. And even though she spoke firmly, Sam could tell that she was rattled. "Obviously. We were playing a little game. Working on our team bonding. And Paige just slipped. She fell into the pool. Maybe her legs cramped up after eating all that pasta. Or she might have hit her head and lost consciousness."

Sam noticed the holes in Bailey's story, the details she'd purposely left out. Like how she'd laughed at Paige. How she hadn't helped her out of the water. How she'd ridiculed the girl and then walked off. But even so, Bailey hadn't been there to witness the worst of it. She hadn't seen Missy in the pool. She hadn't felt her spirit circling, hunting, attacking . . .

"There was something in the water," Sam said, her lips barely moving. But she'd spoken loud enough for Coach Hendricks to hear. For him to take notice and lean in. "Something that dragged Paige under. I tried to help. I tried to pull her up—but I couldn't. I wasn't strong enough. I was too scared. I was afraid that it'd take me down, too." She took a breath, steeling herself for the next part, for what she knew would make her sound ridiculous. She looked to Caroline for support. "Whatever it was, it wasn't human." When Caroline grabbed her hand and squeezed, Sam knew she could say the rest. Knew she had at least one person on her side. "I think it was Missy Caplin's ghost." Sam held her breath as she waited for Coach Hendricks's reply. But he only pulled back, a frown etched on his lips, a tic that she hadn't noticed before pulsing in his jaw. It was clear he hadn't expected to hear that name come out of her mouth. It seemed to disturb him. To make him suddenly uncomfortable.

"Where'd you hear about Missy?" And now it was Coach Hendricks's turn to surprise Sam.

"I told her," Bailey piped up, wedging her way in. "But it was a joke. A story I made up. My sister was on the team with her. She told me about what happened."

"Missy's spirit is real," Sam said, trying her best to stay strong in her convictions. "She was in the water. She grabbed me." And to make it clear that she wasn't delusional, Sam threw off her towel. She showed Coach Hendricks her ankle. The red slashes she'd gotten from Missy's claws. The wounds had started to scab over, but they still throbbed, reminding Sam of how close she'd come to joining Paige.

"I didn't see anything in the pool," Bailey scoffed, unimpressed, acting as if she was jealous of Sam for getting all this attention.

"But I did." Caroline jumped in to defend Sam.

"Of course you did. You're her friend." Bailey rolled her eyes as she turned to Coach Hendricks. "You can't actually believe this. That a dead girl drowned Paige? Ghosts don't exist—"

Bailey cut off as Coach Hendricks raised his hand. "I know that you're probably a little traumatized right now," he began, speaking slowly, choosing his words carefully. "And who wouldn't be after seeing all that. After losing your teammate. Your friend. But . . ." He trailed off, his silence filling in the blank without him having to say it.

"I'm not making it up," Sam murmured, losing confidence as she was ignored, growing slightly angry that Coach

Hendricks wouldn't listen. That he wouldn't believe her. "I'm telling the truth. I promise you."

Another silence stretched to fill the space, to suffocate them all. Then Coach Hendricks sighed and his fingers stopped their drumming. He leaned forward and gave Sam the most pitiful look she'd ever received. "Your dad told me about the lake," Coach Hendricks eventually said, his voice gentle and sad. "About what happened to your friend."

Sam's heart stopped as she realized what he was saying. She swiveled around, her eyes searching for her dad through the glass wall of the office. Coach Hendricks had called him after the accident. He was either on his way or already there. But she didn't need to see his face to confirm that he'd told. That Coach Hendricks knew about Kasey. Sam turned back around and sank deeper into her chair, a flush racing up her cheeks, blazing across her forehead.

"He was worried about you," Coach Hendricks said, reading the betrayal in Sam's body language. "He wanted to protect you. Your best friend drowned right next to you. But you have to know that there was nothing you could have done to save her. Just like there was nothing you could have done to save Paige. You tried your best to help. You can't blame yourself."

Sam only shook her head and retreated deeper into her towel. She wasn't listening. She couldn't. Her head started spinning, and she began to feel dizzy. Nauseated, like she might throw up.

"Sam?" Coach Hendricks's voice broke through the maelstrom and she looked up. Concern knitted his eyebrows together, and for a split second Sam thought he understood. "Now, would you like to tell me what really happened?"

Sam let her breath out. Her shoulders sagged as her whole body deflated, as she realized that it didn't matter what she said. It didn't matter what she'd seen. He was never going to believe her. No one would. He knew about Kasey, so, he saw Sam as fragile. As needing protection. As someone he couldn't trust. And what was worse was that now Bailey knew, too.

"It's like Bailey said," Sam eventually mumbled, her gaze never leaving her lap. "Paige fell in and must have hit her head. I jumped in after her when I realized something was wrong. But I was already too late."

Coach Hendricks nodded, his expression still grave but more relaxed now. It was a story he could wrap his head around. A narrative that made sense. "Thank you for being honest with me. You all hang tight. I'll be right back. The police might want to question you, but I'll tell them what happened. Hopefully, I can make this go away. You girls have already been through enough tonight."

Coach Hendricks didn't wait for an answer as he got up from his desk. As he made his way around the room and slipped out the door.

An uncomfortable quiet fell in his wake. Sam didn't know what to do or how to feel. She was shell-shocked. Hollowed out. Paige was dead—there was no denying that—and Missy had almost gotten her, too. But how could Sam stop anyone else from getting hurt? How could she save them—save herself—if no one believed her? How could she put an end to all of this? And was it even worth the risk of trying?

A hand fell on her knee and Sam glanced up, expecting to see Caroline there, attached to that soothing gesture. But it was Bailey. And for once, the girl didn't look ready to skin her alive. Instead, she looked sad. She looked like she was sorry for Sam. Which might have been worse. Because while Bailey might feel sympathetic for Sam in the moment, eventually the shock and sadness of Paige's death would wear off. Eventually, Bailey would turn what she'd just learned about Sam's past into a weakness. Into a weapon.

But at this point, Sam didn't even know if that mattered. Because the pool wasn't safe—not while Missy was out there. Which left Sam wondering if she'd be able to conquer her fear. If she'd be able to get back in the water.

CHAPTER
FIFTEEN

Music pumped into Sam's ears, drowning out the world around her as she lay on her bed and stared up at the ceiling. In the days following Paige's death, a stillness had settled over her house, uncomfortable and awkward and altogether unheard of. Sam had never felt like she couldn't talk to her dad, and he had never been so lost for what to say to her. They'd been tip-toeing around each other, avoiding the big stuff, letting it steep and simmer and scald.

But how could she talk to him about Paige's death? How could she make him understand that she wasn't only sad but that she was scared, too? Terrified of Missy? Of those claws that had scratched at her leg? That had tried to pull her under after they'd finished off Paige?

She'd tried to tell Coach Hendricks the truth, but he hadn't believed her. No one had, except for Caroline and Duncan.

And now Sam didn't know where to turn. She didn't know who she could trust.

A new song came on and Sam skipped it. The energized beat reminded her of her prerace routine, of the playlists she'd plug in to hype herself up before diving into the pool. It was too sad to think about. Too frightening. And not just because of Missy or her fear of drowning. But because of the loss that it represented.

Sam had always felt her best while swimming, while doing something she was great at. Something she had devoted so much of her life to. But now she didn't know if she'd ever go in the water again. She'd resorted to taking two-minute showers— never a bath—dancing in and out of the spray, her lips sealed tight, her eyes unblinking, always focused on the spigot in case Missy appeared. She hadn't forgotten the bloody bathtub. The wet footprints in her hallway. Missy had already followed her beyond the high school pool, which meant that Sam needed to stay away from all forms of water and limit her exposure.

Luckily, practice had been canceled, the pool closed. So, Sam hadn't had to face her dad or Coach Hendricks yet. She hadn't had to make that decision not to swim. She hadn't had to see her dad crestfallen and disappointed. But eventually, it'd reopen. They'd hold a memorial or a moment of silence for Paige. Then Coach Hendricks would have them back swimming laps like nothing had happened, and everyone would go along with it, forgetting so easily what had happened. Her dad would expect her to pick right back up where she'd left off. Would expect record times and first-place finishes. Would expect nothing less than perfection. Only Sam wouldn't be out there with the rest of the team. She couldn't be. Not with Missy's spirit lurking.

But who was she without swimming? Without the state championships and personal records? Without the pungent aroma of chlorine clinging to her body? The perpetually dry skin and hair, the early morning practices and sore muscles, the red goggle marks ringing her eyes? Without her dad cheering her on from the sidelines, so proud when she won?

"You got a minute?"

Sam jerked as a shadow fell over her, as she realized she wasn't alone. She lifted one ear of her headphones and peeked to the side, spotting her dad standing in the doorway. He hovered there, waiting for a response, for an invitation. And Sam, sensing that she couldn't keep avoiding him for much longer, relented. She nodded and he came inside, stopping after a few steps to stare at her rows of trophies, at the rack of blue-ribbon medals hanging on her wall.

"You have a lot to be proud of," he murmured. "And even more to look forward to." His fingers trembled as he reached for the awards, as his eyes started to shine. But then his face suddenly screwed up into a grimace. His knee buckled, and

Sam thought he might collapse to the floor. At the last second, he caught himself, pushing through the pain, putting on a brave face for Sam, showing her what it meant to be resilient.

"Dad?" Sam asked, sitting up. She pulled her headphones all the way off so that she could hear. She knew better than to ask about his injury. He was too proud for that. He didn't like his weaknesses to be addressed, to be exposed. Which Sam could relate to because she was the same. "Is there something you wanted to talk about?"

His hand darted to the side and rested on the dresser, the anchor giving him stability, extra security for whatever he'd come up here to say. "It's so sad what happened to that girl. Your teammate."

"Paige." Sam filled in the blank. Because she thought Paige deserved at least that much. A name to be remembered by.

"Right. Paige." Her dad continued like he'd known it all along. "I can't imagine what her family's going through. How the other girls on the team are coping. What you must be feeling. Did you know her well?"

Sam couldn't say that she had. But that didn't mean she hadn't been affected by Paige's death. That she wasn't processing it all, too, grieving like everyone else.

"I knew her a little," Sam said, her mouth dry and sticky as she spoke. "We'd talked a couple of times. We were acquainted. Teammates."

Not friends. But Sam *had* been the last one to hear her voice. To feel her pulse. To look into her horrified eyes.

"It was a terrible accident," her dad went on, even as Sam stiffened at his choice in words. "Bad luck and bad timing. And I know you're probably thinking back to Kasey. Back to when you were six. But just like then, this isn't your fault. There's nothing you could have done to prevent it. It actually makes me glad that I got you into swim lessons so early. So that something like this couldn't happen to you."

Sam didn't correct him. She didn't think she could. She didn't want to admit that she was just as vulnerable as Paige. That being a strong swimmer wouldn't save her. Because it hadn't saved Missy. And she'd been almost as fast as Sam. She'd been untouchable in the water. Until she wasn't. Until she'd drowned. It was like Bailey had said. The water could come for anyone. And when it did, all the swim lessons in the world meant nothing.

"Can I ask you something, Dad?" Sam surprised even herself when the words came out of her mouth. "What really happened in the lake, when Kasey drowned?" She'd never asked it so blatantly, but suddenly, she desperately needed to know.

"What do you mean?" Her dad peered at her with puzzled eyes, a little shocked, too, as if he were trying to connect the dots to see the whole picture.

"Did you try to save her, too? Did I?" Sam waited as her

dad took a deep breath. Waited as he composed himself, his grip growing tighter on her dresser, his knuckles turning white.

"I'll never forget that day," he eventually sighed, looking to the ceiling as if he could see into the past. "I'll never forget how scared I was when you didn't come up. When the both of you stayed underwater for so long. You were there one second, and then the next, you were nowhere, like the lake had swallowed you in one gulp."

"But could you see us under the surface?" Sam prompted, needing her dad to finish the whole story. "Was I trying to pull Kasey up?"

Her dad only shook his head, his free hand jumping up to rub his forehead. "The water was so murky. I couldn't see either of you. But there were bubbles, so I jumped in. I swam down as far as I could go and I saw you there. My daughter, trapped in the reeds, scared and sinking."

His face screwed up as he recalled the details, as he thought hard about it. "I only saw you," he finished. "After I pulled you out, I tried going back down. I tried finding Kasey, but she'd been under for too long. She was already gone."

Sam's chin dipped and tears formed in the corners of her eyes.

"But Kasey will always be with you," her dad went on, rushing the words out as he pushed off the dresser and came closer to Sam. He bent down and sat on the edge of the bed, cupping her face in his hand, pulling her eyes up to meet his gaze. He smiled at her and lifted her necklace up to inspect it. To show her what he saw. "As long as you wear her seashell, you won't forget. You'll remember your friend. She's the reason you got in the pool. She's why you're such a strong swimmer. Her memory has driven you to where you are today. And I know she'd be so proud of everything you've become. Of all that you've accomplished and the bright future you still have ahead of you."

Sam gulped, feeling the weight of her dad's words. But the truth of them dragged her down instead of lifting her up. They didn't motivate her. They made her want to run and hide. They made her feel icky. Because how could she have taken something so horrible and seen a silver lining in it? How could she have profited off a tragedy like that?

"Was there something else you wanted?" Sam asked, her voice flat, unfeeling.

"There was, actually." Her dad patted his pockets as if the pantomime would make it clearer. "I just got off the phone with Coach Hendricks and he said the pool is back up and running." He sounded excited, but also like he was trying to hide it, like he knew he shouldn't be.

Sam's expression must have soured because her dad jumped right in to explain.

"They officially ruled Paige's death an accidental

drowning, so you don't need to worry about safety. And they drained the pool. Got it professionally cleaned and refilled."

Sam cringed at the thought of that. Of swimming through particles of Paige's DNA, stray hairs and minute flecks of skin.

"They even rescheduled your first meet. It's in two days."

This news surprised Sam. A competition that soon? What team would want to swim in a pool where someone had just drowned?

"So, do you think you're ready to get back in?" Sam's dad looked at her expectantly, hope twisting in the curve of his lips, lighting up the depths of his eyes. He acted like he had everything riding on her. Which, to some degree, he did. He'd made so many sacrifices over the years, with his job and his free time. He'd paid for swim lessons and driven her to meets every weekend. He'd woken up early to get her to practice on time. He'd bought her new suits and goggles and swim caps. Flippers and kickboards and pull buoys. Everything she needed to be the best. He'd invested in it. In her. This was his dream that had been taken from him when he'd gotten injured. How could she tell him that she didn't want to swim anymore? That she couldn't go back in that pool? How could she disappoint him?

"Your mom will be here for it," Sam's dad added. "She's driving up the morning of the meet. She misses you and can't wait to see you swim. To see all your hard work paying off."

Sam didn't know what to say. She didn't know how to react. She gulped, her tongue sticking to the roof of her mouth. And then, even as her fingers curled into her bedspread and a voice screamed in her head that she was making a mistake, she nodded. She slapped on a fake smile and beamed at her dad. "Of course I'm ready."

And even though she wasn't, she didn't know what else to say.

CHAPTER
SIXTEEN

"I can't believe you're doing this," Caroline exclaimed as she watched Sam pace back and forth on the pool deck. "It's too dangerous. Just tell Coach—"

"Tell him what?" Sam muttered. "That a ghost is haunting the pool? That it's trying to drown me? I tried that and no one believed me."

Caroline changed tactics. "No one's making you swim. You don't have to get in there. You don't have to prove anything to anyone."

"But I do." This Sam said more to herself. "My dad's watching. My mom drove up just to see me swim. Do you know how much they've given up for me? How much I owe them?"

"Supporting your dream shouldn't be transactional."

"We all have this dream," Sam shot back more forcefully

than she meant to. "Getting a scholarship to college. Swimming in the Olympics. It's what we're working toward. It's been the goal since I was six. I can't let it all go to waste."

"But are you sure it's what *you* want? And not what *they* want for you?"

Sam came to a sudden stop, spinning around to face Caroline. "Yes. Of course it's what I want."

And it was, wasn't it?

"What are you going to do if something happens?" Caroline kept at it. "What if you see Missy out there? What if she tries to pull you under again?"

Caroline's questions demanded answers, but Sam didn't know if she had them. The scratch marks on her leg had healed, but she hadn't forgotten their bite, the way Missy had shredded through her skin, almost like the girl's spirit was trying to claw its way into Sam's body, trying to seep into her flesh, to take control. She shuddered as a chill tingled through her, as her breath turned to ice in her lungs. She began to wonder whether she really could do this.

"I just need to be fast," Sam insisted, shaking her head, dispelling her doubts. "And besides, people are watching. Missy hasn't shown herself in front of a crowd like that. And worst-case scenario, the lifeguard will jump in if something happens. If I start to go under."

Sam hoped that was good enough. She only needed to survive for a minute. Less than that, actually. The one-hundred-yard freestyle was one of the quickest races. If she sprinted fast enough, nothing would be able to catch her. Not even Missy.

"But you're swimming in circles," Caroline said, her reason poking holes in Sam's waterproof strategy. "You can't expect to outrun her."

"Well, I guess I'll just have to hope she gets distracted. That she leaves me alone."

Sam huffed, her chin falling against her chest as she tried to focus. Because it wasn't just Missy on her mind. Bailey would be coming for her, too. Sam needed to be at her best. Which she couldn't be if she was worried about what might happen out there. How, if things went wrong, it could be her last race ever.

"I couldn't do it," Caroline murmured, and Sam glanced up, thankful that her friend got it, that she wasn't still trying to convince her not to swim. There was a power in Caroline's admission, in what it said about Sam. Caroline couldn't do it, but Sam could. Or, at least, she was brave enough to try.

"Good thing you have a handy excuse." Sam softened as she gestured to the cast plastered around Caroline's wrist. Caroline hadn't realized it at the time with all the adrenaline coursing through her, but when she'd snatched Sam out of the pool and away from Missy's grip, she'd slammed her hand into the deck so hard that she'd cracked a bone. She'd woken up the next morning with a swollen, throbbing wrist, and now she was out for the season.

"Duncan and I will be watching," Caroline assured Sam. "Just in case the lifeguard is slacking. We'll make sure nothing happens. If Missy comes after you, we'll get you out before it's too late."

Sam didn't know how to say it. She was thankful. Appreciative for her friends, that they were standing by her side. She didn't have to face this alone. "I'm gonna go and clear my head before the race," she said. "Thank you, though. I know you all have my back."

She squeezed Caroline's uninjured hand and looked across the pool, where she spotted Duncan staring at them. He crinkled an eyebrow, and she nodded back, lifting her arm in gratitude. He and Caroline must have gotten together before and made their plan, each of them responsible for patrolling one end of the pool while she swam so someone would be close at all times.

"Be safe." And with that, Caroline let Sam go.

Making her way around the pool, Sam fumbled in her parka jacket, searching for her phone. Her headphones were already looped around her neck, so she only needed to hit play to cue her pump-up playlist. But as she scrolled through the songs, she didn't know what she wanted to listen to. She didn't know what would work to get her ready. This time, she was diving into a completely different kind of race. With a paranoia she'd never had to deal with before. She wasn't sure which song would help block out all those worries. Which would keep her focused. So instead of listening to music, she tried concentrating on her own breathing, on calming her beating pulse. She watched the race in the pool, trying to glean comfort from the fact that nothing seemed to be slowing anyone down. No one else seemed to detect anything amiss. Which meant that maybe it was safe. Maybe Missy was busy somewhere else. Maybe her spirit had only needed the one victim to satisfy itself. Maybe there were too many people around for her to make an appearance. Or maybe she was just lying in wait, sharpening her claws for when Sam entered the water.

"Sam."

She turned at the sound of her name and spotted Assistant Coach Carson there at the edge of the pool, waving her over.

"You heading up for your race? I'll have your splits when you're done. Come find me after and we can go over them. Or, I guess, you can tell me what they mean. I'm still learning about all this."

Sam appreciated that Assistant Coach Carson didn't pretend to know what she was talking about. After all, the woman had never been a star swimmer when she was a student there. But they'd needed a faculty member to supervise the team, to be on the coaching staff as an official representative of the school, and she had volunteered.

"Sounds good," Sam replied, her gaze sliding back to the water, watching it carefully, uneasily.

"It looks like you're in lane five."

Sam jerked her head up when she heard this, her eyebrows furrowed in confusion.

"That's what it says here." The assistant coach fumbled with her heat sheet, smoothing out the crinkles so she could show Sam the lineup.

"Bailey's in three?" Sam asked, unable to hide the outrage in her voice.

It was a dual meet, so the lanes alternated between teams, the home side getting the odd numbers while the visitors got the even. That meant that lane three, the one in the middle of the pool, should have gone to the fastest swimmer on their team. To her. Sam. Lane five was for the runner-up.

"Coach Hendricks gave Bailey three because she's a senior."

"But my time is faster."

The assistant coach shrugged, not understanding why Sam would be upset. "It's just a lane. Aren't they all the same?"

No, they weren't. But before Sam could launch into an explanation of why she deserved the top spot, someone came up and tapped the assistant coach on the shoulder, and Sam was surprised by how startled Assistant Coach Carson seemed when she turned and saw who it was.

"I didn't realize you were working with the swim team," said the woman, who looked to be about the same age as Assistant Coach Carson. "I kind of don't believe it. You never seemed to like the water much."

"And from what I recall," the assistant coach hissed through clenched teeth, "neither did you."

The women glowered at each other, locked in a standoff that Sam didn't understand.

"I'm Jenna, by the way." The woman turned to face Sam, ignoring Assistant Coach Carson's remark, and extended her hand. "Bailey's older sister."

Sam sucked in a breath as she shook the hand that had been offered to her. As she took note of the similarities between the woman and Bailey. Between her and the little girl Sam had seen in Missy's memory.

So, this was Bailey's sister. According to Bailey, she had been best friends with Missy and had quit the team after the girl's death. But Sam knew that was wrong. She knew that Jenna was actually one of Missy's tormentors. One of her bullies. Making the sisters not all that different.

"I love your necklace," Jenna said, not waiting for Sam to reply. "Where'd you get it?"

Sam touched her chest, only now realizing that she'd forgotten to take it off.

"I found it," she replied. "At the bottom of the pool."

Assistant Coach Carson and Jenna both paused as they looked closer at Sam's jewelry, as something like recognition flashed across their faces.

"Your bracelet's really cute, too," Sam said, feeling the need to return the compliment. She didn't particularly like the string of black beads Jenna had wrapped around her wrist, but it was polite and an easy out.

"Just a little good luck charm," Jenna said, flicking her hand so that the light caught the beads. But instead of reflecting it back, their dark, bottomless depths seemed to swallow it whole. "I got really into crystals during college. These are black tourmaline. They're supposed to ward off evil spirits."

Sam nodded, thinking that she could use that bracelet right about now.

"Jenna and I went to high school together," Assistant Coach Carson broke in, answering the question Sam hadn't gotten around to asking. "But that was a long time ago."

"Speaking of . . ." Jenna let her words trail off, her eyes darting to the pool. Or had Sam imagined that?

"I've got a meet to get back to." Assistant Coach Carson shook her stopwatch at Jenna. "Splits to record."

"Another time, then," Jenna said after a moment, the smile she'd worn during the entire exchange suddenly slipping away. "I'll be around."

"Jenna—" Sam tried to get the woman's attention. This was the first person she'd come across who'd actually known Missy. Who could tell her more about what had happened back then. But Bailey's sister had already gone, leaving Sam's tongue tied with the questions she so desperately needed answers to.

"Coach?" Sam said, turning to the other woman, looking to get answers from her instead.

"You better get to the blocks." Assistant Coach Carson didn't even glance up as she scribbled something down on her heat sheet, and Sam realized she wouldn't get anything out of her either. At least not right now. But she knew who to come to later. Knew she might be able to find something out. If she didn't miss her race. If she made it through unscathed.

As Sam cut a path to the start, she steered clear of the water, giving it as wide a berth as possible. They'd only opened the pool that afternoon, just in time for the meet, so she hadn't swum in over a week. But she wasn't worried about forgetting how. She wasn't worried that her arms wouldn't move fast enough or that her muscles would stop firing. Swimming lived in her bones. The strokes and kicks would come back to her. She just had to get it all started. Dive in and her body would take over.

"That's my lane," Bailey sniped as she sauntered up, delight all over her face.

Sam jumped out of the way, only realizing then that she'd settled behind lane three. "Sorry. Old habit, I guess," she said. "But I wouldn't get used to it." And Sam hoped that she'd sounded just as confident as Bailey. Just as vile.

Moving behind her actual lane assignment, Sam stuffed her towel into an empty chair. She shed her parka and tossed it on top, hoping she'd make it out so she could slip it on again, feel the warmth wrap around her shoulders, hugging her tight.

She tried to stick to her prerace routine, shaking out her

arms, hyping herself up by jumping and slapping her legs. She wiped her goggles clean and pressed them to her face, adjusting the straps around her head until they felt snug.

The whistle trilled, and it was her turn to swim. She moved up to the block and stood there, her gaze drifting down the pool. She saw her parents first. They'd gotten pom-poms from somewhere and shook them at her, excitement pulsing off them, not an ounce of nerves in their cheers. Then Sam spotted Caroline and Duncan posted up on either side of the pool, their eyes glued to her, tracing her every step.

She blew out a long exhale. She could do this. She'd done it more times than she could count. She needed to remember that.

As the whistle blew again, Sam stepped up on the block, her head bowed to the water, only seconds away from diving in. Her legs quivered as the starter called them to their marks. As she bent over and grabbed the edge of the block.

She gulped in a last breath, and then the starting tone sounded. The race began.

CHAPTER
SEVENTEEN

The high-pitched squeal of the starter's horn reverberated in Sam's ears, piercing her to the core. She crouched on the block, frozen in place, watching as her competitors moved in slow motion around her, leaping headfirst into the water, leaving her behind.

Hundredths of a second, and then tenths, ticked by, as she lost her ground little by little, digging a hole until her brain finally connected with her muscles. Until her thighs tensed, her arms yanked back, and she exploded off the block.

Sam seemed to hang in the air forever, her hands stretched out in front of her like a superhero, straining to keep her aloft, to keep her safe and sound and dry. For a moment, she even thought she could fly. That she'd never come down. But that was all a trick. Wishful thinking. As gravity asserted itself on Sam's shoulders, she jackknifed, bending at the waist, repositioning her body into a straight line, an arrow that hit the surface of the pool and broke through in one clean hole, her momentum torpedoing her through the water, catching her up an inch at a time.

As Sam charged down the pool, she didn't think. Adrenaline poured into her bloodstream, firing her up, making her feel invincible. The one-hundred freestyle was made up of four twenty-five-yard lengths, each of which should take Sam just under thirteen seconds to complete. An unlucky number, for sure. But a fast one, too. Exactly what she needed. Hitting the first wall, she flipped and pushed off. One turn down, two to go.

As Sam made her way through the race, she tried to keep focused on what was right in front of her. She followed the black stripe on the bottom of the pool, the line running through the center of her lane. She stuck to it, taking the shortest route possible, not swimming in circles like they did in practice, making sure she didn't add unnecessary inches to her race. She also tried to stay within herself. She couldn't use up all her energy early or she would gas out. But she still had a deficit to make up, and each time she breathed toward the center of the pool, she couldn't help but notice Bailey there ahead of her.

Two turns in, and Sam was still half a body length behind. She couldn't remember the last time she'd trailed at the halfway point. The last time she'd felt this kind of pressure. Felt like she might lose. She kept swimming, though, kept grinding away. She could still do this. She could still win.

But with each passing second, Sam grew more tired. The initial injection of adrenaline had burned off and her thoughts started to creep in: paranoia that Missy was down there, waiting to strike. The worries crowded against her skull and made it hard to concentrate. She felt like she was taking on water, filling up slowly but surely. Any second now the balance would tip and she'd sink under. She felt safest whenever she reached the shallow end. It was harder—though not impossible—to drown in three feet of water. But she knew she couldn't linger there. Not if she wanted to catch Bailey. Not if she wanted to win. And she needed to do both.

Sam rounded the last turn and pushed home, pouring everything she had left into it. Her arms ached as they dug through the water. Her legs screamed as the lactic acid built up, as her quads started to seize. She was breathing on every other stroke, her lungs on fire, her body desperate for oxygen. And even with all that, it wasn't enough. She wasn't catching Bailey. She wasn't gaining any ground. They were barreling toward the end of the race, and Sam was running out of time. It didn't look good for her, but she wouldn't give up. She kept pushing, her stroke growing frantic, her arms flailing wildly. She rotated her head to take in a breath and inhaled a gush of water, choking on it, hacking as the liquid flooded her lungs.

She started coughing, gasping for air even though none

could make it through. Even though her mouth and throat and lungs were only taking on more water. She tried to swim through it, but there was no point. No use. She'd slowed down. Lost her momentum. Lost her chance.

Glancing to the side, Sam saw Bailey's legs kicking away. Saw the girl's feet churning up the water, propelling her to the finish. To victory.

It was too late; Sam couldn't win. And as she realized this, she noticed a shadow creeping up on her. Cruising along right behind her. She felt a cold pull. Felt fingers tickling her toes and climbing up her legs.

Sam's chest constricted as fear gripped her, as an underwater scream threatened to burst from her mouth. She hadn't thought her body could feel more pain, but this was a different kind. It ran deeper than her muscles. It burrowed into her bones, hollowing her out, breaking her into pieces. Because Missy was here. And she had her sights set on her next victim.

Glancing ahead, Sam watched as Bailey accelerated. As she sprinted into the wall and finished strong. When she touched in first place, all the fight went out of Sam. The power and the drive. It just disappeared, leaving her dead in the water.

Sam shook her head and tried to make sense of it. But her thoughts had grown fuzzy. There was still water in her lungs, and when she reopened her eyes, she couldn't exactly see straight. She couldn't think. She couldn't keep her arms moving. She couldn't kick. A claw scratched up her leg, opening her up, making her want to wail.

She slowed and then stopped. She floated there as darkness swam at the edge of her vision, murky water closing in. Her chest ached, but she didn't know why. She could barely feel the pain anymore. Could hardly feel anything. She was so tired. So over being afraid. Of Bailey. Of losing. Of disappointing her parents. Of drowning. It was all too much. So, as the darkness washed over her, Sam gave in. She surrendered to it. She let it take her somewhere else.

Blinking, Sam realized that she was back at the Wentworth Public Pool. It must have been the end of summer because the bubble wasn't up. Instead, a gray sky hung overhead, a downpour in motion as rain pummeled the pool's surface. A lone figure swam through the middle lane, its stroke steady and quick, cutting through the water above and below like it was nothing, refusing to slow down at all.

"Suck-up!" someone called from the deck, and Sam had to strain her eyes to see the cluster of swimmers huddled under one of the big sun umbrellas, shivering in their swimsuits. "Coach's pet."

Sam homed in on the person speaking and wasn't surprised to find that it was Jenna, a teenage version of her this time. Maybe thirteen or fourteen.

"She's trying to make us all look bad," Jenna muttered, her fists clenching, her gaze trained on Coach Hendricks, who was standing on the other side of the pool under a different umbrella, his eyes glued to his stopwatch.

Sam figured that the rest of the team must have taken cover when the rain had started. But as long as there wasn't thunder or lightning, it was safe to swim, practice could go on as scheduled, which was what it looked like Missy was doing. Getting her laps in. Staying ahead. It was what a champion would do. What Sam would have done, too.

Jenna kept up her attack. "She thinks she's so much better than us. I don't care how fast she is or how many races she wins, she's a freak and she shouldn't get too cocky."

This got a laugh out of the rest of the team, which made Sam queasy, seeing how easy it was to turn a group against someone else, to have them all gang up on poor, lonely Missy.

"Let's get back to practice," Coach Hendricks barked, his sudden command making some of the swimmers jump. "I promise you it's warmer in the water than out. Just look at Missy. She's not letting it bother her. Mind over matter, folks. Mind over matter."

"Just look at Missy," Jenna mimicked as she reluctantly pulled her goggles on and prepared to head out into the rain. "I'm so sick of it. I wish someone would just put her in her place."

And then an idea seemed to strike. A wicked grin flitted onto her lips, and she turned to whisper into one of the boy swimmer's ears. She wiggled her fingers and he continued to pass whatever she'd told him on to another boy, and then another.

As the team walked out from under the umbrella, worry collected in the pit of Sam's stomach. She didn't want to see what happened next. Was this the day that Missy drowned? Was this how it ended?

Reaching the shallow end of the pool, the boys lined up in a row. For some reason, they seemed to be waiting to dive back in, to start their next set. At the same time, Missy had reached the middle of the pool and was cutting her way toward them, toward her next flip turn.

Too late, Sam realized what they had planned. She threw her hand up and tried to shout, tried to warn Missy even though she knew the girl couldn't hear her. Knew that she couldn't change a memory. She could only watch it unfold, her heart in her throat, her body shivering with dread.

As Missy came into the wall, the three boys on the deck crouched and wound their arms back, loading up their legs. Then, as one, they launched themselves into the pool, a triangle of cannonballs creating craters in the water, all of them inches from an unsuspecting Missy.

The impact caused Missy to veer off course. Sent her careening into the lane line, a head-on collision. She jumped to her feet, choking, gasping for breath. She snatched her goggles from her face and glared at the boys, but they seemed completely unbothered as they broke out into more laughter and pushed off into their set.

Fury reddening her cheeks, Missy turned to Coach Hendricks on the deck, but he was absorbed in his clipboard, purposely ignoring the altercation in the pool, doing the same nothing that he had done for Sam and Duncan.

"Gotta be prepared for anything," Jenna said, standing above Missy, drawing her attention. Then, without another word, she dove into the pool, sailing over Missy's head, her splash kicking up into the girl's face, an added insult.

See what they did to me? How they treated me?

Sam snapped around as a voice spoke into her ear.

They'll never change as long as they can get away with it.

Sam nodded, because it was true. Bailey. Jenna. Clark. Keith. Even Paige. They all were bullies. And no one was doing anything to stop them.

Let me help you.

We'll show them what their cruelty feels like.

We'll make them pay.

CHAPTER
EIGHTEEN

Sam gasped, cold air hitting her lungs, shocking her system. She coughed and water sputtered out of her mouth, splashing onto the ground beside her with a sickeningly satisfying noise. Light stabbed into her eyes, peeled her lids open, stinging, singeing, too bright after that vast black void. She blinked, forgetting. Forgetting where she was. Who she was. What had happened.

She lay in a puddle, chilly tiles pressing into her back, her fingertips starting to prune. A man knelt over her, his arm on her shoulder, shaking her as water dripped from his clothes. As it hit her like sprinkles of rain.

"Sam? Can you hear me?"

Was that her name?

His voice came to her from so far away, echoing like it had traveled through a long tunnel just to reach her. She shook her head and felt droplets writhing around in her head, sliding across her eardrums, a soft shushing. She parted her lips, but she couldn't seem to make a noise. Couldn't seem to make herself heard. Even though she was waterlogged, her throat was parched. Dry and brittle. A husk.

She took in another breath, feeling it rattle in her chest. She shivered and the man suddenly had a towel in his hands. He wrapped it around her shoulders, his touch gentle but firm. He rubbed her arms in circles, encouraging the blood to circulate, to disperse warmth and oxygen throughout her body.

"Just breathe for me," he said, and suddenly a memory knocked loose in her head, resurfacing from a long time ago. This same man standing over her as she lay on wooden planks, the rough grain of the dock biting into her skin, grounding her, bringing her back from the brink.

"Dad?" she croaked. And by the way his face lit up, she knew she was right. "What happened?"

"You almost drowned," he replied calmly, speaking as if it were a common enough occurrence. As if Sam hadn't almost died. "But I got you. I always will."

"But—" Sam's thoughts started to come back to her. "But did you see her? Did you see Missy? She was in the water. She tried to pull me under."

Sam watched her dad take a deep breath. Watched and waited for him to say that he'd seen Missy, too. That he believed her. But as he struggled to find an answer to her question, she began shaking her head, knowing she wasn't going to like what he had to say.

"It was just you in the water, honey," her dad explained, speaking slowly like she'd had a concussion or just woken up from a coma.

"No, no, no, no," Sam muttered, trying to drown him out, to hold tight to the truth she knew.

"You were swimming along in your race just fine," her dad went on, talking over her droning. "And then, suddenly, you started flailing. You couldn't hear us trying to calm you down. We were trying to get you to grab on to the lane line or swim to the wall. But you must have worn yourself out. Swallowed too much water. You began sinking. That's when I jumped in to get you."

"No!" Sam shouted, because she didn't know what else to say. Missy had been there. She'd overtaken her. Why hadn't he seen it? Why hadn't anyone noticed? Could Missy cloak herself? Could her spirit go invisible, blend in with the water?

Sam's gaze darted to the puddle beneath her, as if there might be a clue hidden there. A trace of something. Of Missy. A window into her world. But it was only the pool deck, a reflection of the ceiling.

She racked her brain and tried to remember. Tried to recall those last moments in the pool before she'd blacked out. But it was all a blur. A wash of images that she couldn't pick apart. A memory she'd fallen into. Another incident of bullying. Missy alone. A target. No one stepping in to help her. Jenna and those boys getting away with it, free to continue their torment unchecked.

"Did I do that?" Sam had gotten distracted, noticing the bruise forming under her dad's eye. She reached up to touch the same spot on her own face, her skin cold and clammy.

"You got in a good whack or two. But I'll heal. You didn't know what you were doing. I think—I think you were having a panic attack."

He'd paused before finishing, licking his lips nervously as his gaze softened around her.

A panic attack?

The words sent a shiver through Sam. Her heartbeat picked up, beating against her rib cage as if the very mention of panic was now inducing it. Her breathing came in short, quick bursts, her lungs constricting as if they were curling in on themselves.

"It's a totally natural response." Her dad had his hand on her shoulder again, his arm pressing down, holding her in place. Keeping her together. "You've been under a lot of stress lately. Especially after everything that happened with Paige. It's only natural that it might have dredged up memories of Kasey. It's your first time back in the water. We should have known to be more careful. We should have taken it slower. But we'll get you through this. We can set you up with a therapist or a sports psychologist. I'm sure Coach Hendricks has some-one he can recommend. It's going to be fine, you'll see. We'll get you right back on track in no time."

Sam pushed up onto her hands, the string of syllables com-ing out of her dad's mouth too much for her to process. She didn't know what it all meant. How her dad expected things to get better. How a therapist would help. She needed a ghost hunter. Or an exorcist. Not a sports psychologist.

"I can't—" Sam sputtered.

"You don't need to worry."

"No. I'm serious." Sam jerked out of her dad's hold, shak-ing him off, her voice rising as she grew more agitated. Only then did she realize that a crowd had formed around them. Her mom and some of the other parents. Caroline and Duncan and Bailey. They were all watching her. Gawking. Waiting for her to finish. Usually, this kind of attention would have made her anxious. But she wanted them to hear. She wanted to make herself absolutely clear. She needed witnesses.

"I know you're trying to relive your glory days with me," she said to her dad. "To somehow fulfill the dreams that your injury sidelined. But I can't do it anymore. I won't. I quit."

CHAPTER
NINETEEN

"Practice isn't the same without you," Duncan said as he flopped into a chair and unslung his backpack. "Without either of you."

He glanced back and forth between Caroline and Sam, his frown saying it all.

"It must be hard to eat breakfast alone," Caroline joked. "With no one there to save you a vegetarian bagel."

"Truly unbearable." His frown deepened in exaggeration, and Caroline laughed, Duncan breaking a few seconds later. Sam sat there stoically, though, her mind somewhere else as she chewed on the end of her pen.

"Bailey's become a monster," Duncan offered, directing it at Sam, speaking carefully as he tried to get her engaged. "She's pretty satisfied with herself. Telling everyone that she beat you. Acting like she ran you off the team. Like she scared you away."

Sam's eyes darted to Duncan, but she didn't say anything. Didn't show an ounce of emotion.

"How's your dad taking it?" he tried again. "I figured he'd be all over you to get back in the pool."

"He is." Sam finally broke, her voice low and heavy. Exhausted. "He told me that I was giving up. That I was wasting my potential. That he couldn't believe I'd talked to him like that in front of everyone."

Sam did feel guilty about that. She hadn't meant to bring up his injury. How he'd had to quit. The thing that he saw as his biggest failure. She knew he was sensitive about it. It was a low blow and she knew it. But she'd also known that it was the only thing she could have said to make him listen.

"But my mom," Sam picked back up. "She talked to him. She made him back off. For now, at least. I think he's still hoping I'll come around. He's waiting for me to realize how much I miss swimming."

"*Do* you miss it?" Duncan's question hung in the air, floating over the table, over their open textbooks and unfinished homework. It'd only been a few days since Sam's panic attack—since she'd nearly drowned—and practice had ground on like normal. Only without Sam. She'd kept her promise. She'd quit. For good.

"I—I'm not sure," Sam finally said. Which was the truth.

She didn't miss the early morning practices and perpetually

itchy skin. The chlorine smell that clung to her throughout the day. But there was a serenity that washed over her when she was in the pool. A lightness of body and mind as she glided through the water, her muscles working in time, moving together, the world outside muffled, her vision narrowed to the lane in front of her. It was a sensation that made her happy. That made her feel at peace. But Missy had ruined it. The fear of being dragged under. The panic. It'd taken that tranquility and turned it into terror. It'd made Sam worry that she'd never be safe in the water again.

But was that the only reason? If Missy hadn't shown up, would everything have been fine? Would she have been able to go on swimming like normal?

The more Sam thought about it, the more doubts she had. If she was honest with herself, the rivalry with Bailey had made everything harder. That pressure to perform, to excel, to win—it had taken some of the joy away. It had made it so that she was terrified of losing and only relieved when she won. Because it didn't matter how many times she came in first place—if she lost *once*, then she failed. She disappointed. She'd never hear the end of it.

"Why do *you* swim?" Sam asked Duncan, not exactly sure where she was going with the question. "I mean, why not quit? Don't the other guys make it pretty miserable for you? And you're not exactly winning out there."

Duncan's eyes bugged out at Sam's bluntness. At her

rudeness. But she didn't care. She was too exhausted to worry about being delicate.

"First of all," Duncan snapped, pushing a stray lock of his hair back in place, "I shouldn't have to quit because my teammates are bullies. They shouldn't get to dictate whether I swim. That's my choice." He took a deep breath before barreling on. "And secondly, I don't need to be the best to want to do something. I have personal goals. I have reasons to be in that pool that don't hinge on whether or not I come in first place."

That last bit hit Sam hard. It wedged in under her rib cage like a side stitch, sharp and painful, making it difficult to breathe. "You're right. You're right," she rushed out, wincing as she apologized, as she realized what she'd said and how much it must have hurt him. "I didn't mean it like that. I'm sorry. It's just—" She broke off, not sure where to go with her thoughts. Not sure how to articulate them. "I feel so messed up right now. So lost. And I don't know how to fix it."

Silence fell among them as they all thought it over. As everyone struggled with what to say next.

"It sounds like you do miss the pool," Caroline finally whispered, her hand reaching out to pat Sam's. "Like you want to get back in the water."

Sam could only shrug. Because she really didn't know. There was something about not having the choice, though. If she quit swimming, she wanted it to be on her own terms. She didn't want to be forced into it because she was scared. But at the same time, if she tried to get back in the pool, Missy would come for her. She already had. It was too dangerous. And Sam didn't know how to get rid of her. How to banish Missy's ghost or set her soul at peace. She'd gotten flashes of Missy's memories, but she didn't know what to do with them. She wasn't a medium. She didn't know the first thing about dealing with paranormal activity. She could corner Jenna and Assistant Coach Carson and demand that they tell her more about Missy, but would they be honest with her? Would they even know what had actually happened?

No. Sam had run out of ideas. She was tired. Her spirit had been broken. She didn't want to fight anymore. She just wanted peace. She set her head on the table and closed her eyes, defeat sinking into her bones.

"I think I'm done," she said without looking up, unable to take the pained expressions she knew were on her friends' faces.

"Are you sure?" Caroline asked.

"I am," Sam replied after a few more seconds of thought. "I'm positive. I'll go by the locker room tomorrow and clean my things out. This is it for me. Truly."

CHAPTER
TWENTY

The locker room stood empty as Sam stole inside. She'd staked it out all morning, hiding around the corner until she'd counted the whole team heading for breakfast. She didn't want to run into anyone while she cleaned out her things. She didn't want witnesses to her admission of defeat.

Making a beeline across the room, Sam got to her locker and started putting in her combination. She worked fast, spinning through the numbers. She didn't like being even this close to the pool. No one had reported a Missy sighting in the days since Sam had quit, but she could sense the girl's spirit out there waiting for her. Waiting to strike again. It was like Missy's ghost was somehow tied to Sam. Their fates intertwined. Maybe because they shared a similar past. They were the fastest on the team. They'd been bullied mercilessly by girls like Jenna and Bailey.

Sam hadn't forgotten Missy's words to her during those visions, offering her the seeds of revenge. But she couldn't stoop to Bailey's level. She couldn't hurt another person. Perhaps her quitting would keep everyone else safe. Perhaps giving up the water was the sacrifice that Sam needed to make.

Sam shook her head and tried not to think about it. She kept moving, focusing on what she'd come here for. As she opened her locker, the memory of those dead fish flashed in her mind. It seemed so long ago now, but it didn't scare her. Not anymore. She knew Bailey's tricks. She'd grown used to them. Expected them, even. Luckily, she'd no longer have to deal with her. She wouldn't have to watch her back and her front. She wouldn't have to take any more verbal assaults. She was done with swimming, which meant that she was done with Bailey. The bully wouldn't have any reason to bother her now.

A muffled voice filtered through from the hallway and gave Sam a warning that someone was approaching, but she didn't have enough time to hide. Instead, she spun around right as the locker room door swung open and she came face-to-face with Bailey.

"What the hell are you doing in here?" Bailey asked, her eyebrow cocked as if she'd caught Sam breaking and entering.

"Don't worry," Sam replied. "I'm not booby-trapping

your locker or anything." She stared down Bailey for a beat, hoping that the girl would feel a little bad about what she'd done to Sam all those weeks ago. But not an ounce of remorse flashed across her face. Not a shred of apology. "Where did you get those fish heads anyway," Sam asked, nodding toward her open locker as if they were still there. "Did you buy them yourself? Or did you have one of your minions pick them up?"

"I don't know what you're talking about." Bailey crossed her arms over her chest, her lips pressing into a prim and proper smile.

"Whatever," Sam muttered, rolling her eyes and turning back to her locker. It wasn't like it mattered anymore. "I'll be out of your hair soon enough. I'm just here to clean out my stuff and go."

"You're quitting?" Bailey seemed surprised by Sam's official announcement. And maybe a little disappointed. Sam couldn't tell exactly, but the girl's shoulders had slouched the tiniest bit and her voice had fallen flat at the end.

"Congratulations, you're now the fastest girl on the team." Sam knew she sounded bitter, but she was. She wasn't giving up swimming because she wanted to. She had been driven to it. And despite everything that was going on with Missy, Bailey was a part of that decision, too.

"But I didn't—"

"Don't deny it," Sam cut her off, slamming her locker door,

the bang sounding like an explosion in the empty room. "It's what you wanted. Me off the team. You back on top. You'd rather bully me than try and beat me in a fair race. Which is fine. You do what you have to do."

"You're quitting because you can't handle a little competition." Bailey pushed back, recovering the venom she'd lost for just a moment. "You're quitting because you can't handle losing. Because I beat you."

"You didn't beat me." Sam didn't know why she was engaging Bailey like this. Why she'd let the girl draw her into a confrontation. Her plan had been to get in and get out. To avoid a fight. To put this all behind her.

"Yes, I did," Bailey replied coolly, taking a step toward Sam, leaving only a few inches of empty space between them. "And you had to fake a panic attack because you couldn't handle it. Because you couldn't cope with the fact that you lost. To me."

And then, to punctuate the whole thing, Bailey laughed. Right in Sam's face. A short, shrill burst of glee.

Don't let her win.

The thought snaked into Sam's head, dripping down her ear canal, galvanizing her.

Show her what you're made of.

Bailey giggled again, but this time Sam had had enough. Her arms shot out and connected with Bailey's chest. She kept shoving her until she had her pinned up against a wall of lockers, the hollow metal clanging as Bailey's shoulder blades made contact.

"What are you doing?" Bailey shouted, her hair falling in her face as fear flashed in her eyes.

"Standing up for myself," Sam shot back. "Standing up for everyone you've bullied. I won't be a victim anymore."

Bailey's eyes bulged.

Sam cocked her fist back and shot it forward. She slammed it into the locker, making sure that she'd been close enough for Bailey to feel the wind from her punch. Angry tears streaked down her cheeks, but she didn't move to wipe them away. She let them run. Let Bailey see just how upset she was.

Confusion froze Bailey's face, twisting her eyebrows and mouth and forehead and nose into an abstract painting.

"I'm not a bully," she eventually mumbled.

And now it was Sam's turn to laugh.

"Really? You don't think so?"

"I'm not," Bailey said, stomping her foot, doubling down.

"Keep telling yourself that. You're just like your sister. If you're not careful, someone else is going to end up dead." Sam's arms dropped to her sides, but her eyes stayed glued on Bailey, kept her pinned to the lockers with their intensity.

Silence welled up to fill the void left by Sam's words. Somewhere in the middle of all of it, Bailey's mouth had fallen open, her tongue flashing bright pink, the saliva drying with each passing second. Eventually, she closed her mouth and swallowed. She licked her lips and leaned in close. Because it wouldn't be Bailey unless she got the last word in. Unless she tried to come out on top.

"I'm not the one who let Paige die. Who let her best friend drown when she was six."

Bailey's words hit Sam like a blow to the stomach. She doubled over, leaning against the locker for support. Bailey moved around her, that confident swagger back in her walk, and she started heading for the door.

Don't let her win.

The voice slid back into Sam's head and her hand clenched into a fist. She was tired of losing. Tired of letting Bailey beat her down. She wasn't going to let the bully get away with it again.

Spinning around, Sam tracked Bailey as she made her way across the room. She took aim. Then she launched herself at the girl, tackling her from behind, knocking her to the ground. She scrambled on top and held her down. She pinned the girl to the floor even as Bailey bucked, fighting with everything she had.

"Get off me!" Bailey shouted.

"Not until you say you're sorry."

Sam's teeth ground into each other as she tried to hold on. But Bailey was strong. And determined. And really mad. She managed to wedge a knee under Sam's stomach and pried herself free. She started crawling away, but Sam reached out and grabbed her ankle. She tripped her as she tried to get back up.

"Let go of me," Bailey shouted as she kicked herself loose, as she stumbled away and ran into the sinks.

"Not as much fun when someone fights back," Sam admonished, her breath coming in short gasps, her rage evening out as she pulled herself back under control. She didn't know what had come over her. It scared her a little, but it had felt so good to make Bailey squirm, to see her on the receiving end of a fight.

"Stay away from me," Bailey said, the words breaking in her mouth. "Leave me alone."

And then, without even stopping to check her hair and makeup in the mirror, Bailey rushed out into the hallway. She didn't give Sam a second look.

"Good riddance," Sam murmured to the empty locker room.

Sam went back to her locker and opened it. She glanced through her swimsuits and goggles and caps. She read through the inspirational quotes she'd cut out and reminded herself of the goal times she'd circled. She paused on the photos of her and her dad, smiling after she'd won her state championships the year before. She'd hung the pictures up for motivation when practices were hard, when she felt like giving up.

And suddenly, she wasn't so sure about quitting.

Her mind raced as she thought through everything. As she tried to come up with a plan. She could handle Bailey. She knew that now. But what about Missy? She still didn't know exactly what had happened to the girl. How she had drowned. If it had been an accident or something worse. But she knew someone who might know. She knew who she needed to speak to next.

CHAPTER
TWENTY-ONE

"Is it okay if I come in for a minute?"

Sam hovered at the open door of the classroom, her hand still up after she'd knocked. Behind her desk, Assistant Coach Carson set down her coffee and wiped her lips. She hastily closed the book she'd been looking at and motioned for Sam to come in.

"Of course. I was actually hoping to talk to you. To see how you were doing."

Sam wavered for a second. She hadn't come here to open up about herself—about her panic attack and quitting the team—but she might have to open up if she wanted Assistant Coach Carson to do the same. if she wanted to get answers. After all, she had gone to school with Missy. She would know more than anyone what had happened ten years ago. She could help make sense of it all.

Slipping into the room, Sam took a seat in the front row, facing Assistant Coach Carson at her desk. The walls were papered over with blown-up book covers, Shakespearean tragedies and coming-of-age classics. Sam was staring up at an illustration of a ghostly king haunting a young man when Assistant Coach Carson got her attention.

"How have you been holding up?"

"Fine," Sam mumbled, answering quickly, keeping it short as her eyes darted away and landed on another poster, this one depicting a grayed-out woman watching over two frightened children.

"You've been swimming your whole life and now you've stopped," the woman pressed on, not letting Sam off the hook. "I'd expect you to feel something. Sadness? Or maybe relief?"

She wasn't falling for Sam's act. Which meant that Sam had to give her something.

"It's hard," Sam said, scooting her desk forward, closing the gap between them. "I feel lost. But also . . . free. Like, swimming was something that anchored me in place. Something I felt a security in. I knew where I was going. But now that I've cut myself loose, I'm just kind of floating. And I have no clue where I'll end up. Either it'll be someplace great or someplace terrible. But it's guaranteed to be a surprise."

"As an English teacher, I appreciate the metaphor." Assistant Coach Carson smirked, and Sam knew she'd won some brownie points. "But you know you've still got time. This isn't it."

"It was for Paige." Sam hadn't meant to bring it up, but the words slipped out before she realized it, the sentiment behind them terrible and true.

"Paige's death was a tragedy. But it wasn't your fault. You know that, right? You don't have to give up swimming because she drowned."

"That's not why I quit," Sam sputtered, feeling herself start to lose control.

"You can't blame yourself for what happened to her. You shouldn't."

"But I could have saved her." This, Sam suddenly realized, was what had been gnawing away at her for weeks. The fear that she could be next, sure. But also, this. Survivor's guilt. The why-her-and-not-me. It had been the same when she was six. Why had Kasey drowned when she'd been saved? Was it just dumb luck? Fate?

"If I'm such a good swimmer"—Sam's words spilled out as she strung together the thought—"then why didn't I pull her out?"

"Sometimes it's not in our control. Terrible things happen and there's nothing we can do to stop them. It's a part of life."

"And death." Sam slumped, her head falling onto the desk, her arms covering her face as she held in a sob.

"I lost a friend when I was around your age," Assistant

Coach Carson said quietly, her words delicate, chosen carefully. "And it took me a long time to come to terms with it."

Sam lifted her chin slowly, squinting through teary eyes. She'd forgotten why she'd come in here in the first place. But now Assistant Coach Carson had brought it up. She'd led her right where she wanted to go.

"You kind of remind me of her, actually," Assistant Coach Carson added, lost in her own memories.

"Was it Missy?" Sam asked. And when her assistant coach didn't answer, she pressed on. "I know she was on the team with Bailey's sister. And at the meet you said you'd gone to high school with her."

Assistant Coach Carson fidgeted in her chair. Her face suddenly paled and she looked like maybe she'd seen a ghost.

Sam recognized the opening and leaned in. "What happened to her? How'd she really drown?"

Assistant Coach Carson closed her eyes. She shook her head, as if struggling to remember, as if it pained her to recall it. Then she broke, a sigh escaping her lips, her shoulders slumping as she crumpled in front of Sam.

"Jenna Bailey. Missy Caplin. Kayla Carson." The assistant coach lifted her hand and opened the book that she'd snapped shut when Sam had come in. "We were all in homeroom together. Through middle school and into our freshman year."

She flipped to a page and Sam realized, as rows of black-and-white photos flashed by, that it was an old yearbook.

"Here we are," Assistant Coach Carson said as she stopped on a page. And right there, in the middle of it, was Missy, the same photo Sam had seen in the articles she'd found online, the one that had accompanied her obituary. "And there's me. And Jenna Miller."

The assistant coach pointed to either side of Missy, at younger versions of the women Sam knew as adults.

"But Missy and Jenna weren't friends, were they?" Sam asked, already knowing the answer but wanting confirmation.

"No. Not at all." Assistant Coach Carson scoffed. "They were enemies. Jenna was—she was a bully. She picked on Missy relentlessly. I saw it with my own eyes. And Missy would tell me about it afterward. She would cry and cry and cry. But she refused to tell anyone. Refused to get the principal involved."

"But why did she put up with it? Why didn't she just quit?"

"Because she wanted to be the best. Because she couldn't give up the thing that she loved most." And here, Assistant Coach Carson realized that she'd probably said too much. That she shouldn't have shared all this with a student. "But that was a long time ago. And you know you can always come to me if the girls on the team are bullying you. I'm here for you. Here to protect you. To make sure that something like what happened to Missy doesn't happen to you. Coach Hendricks can be a bit old-school—don't ask, don't tell—but there are ways around him. Ways to get you help if you need it."

"I'm fine," Sam exclaimed, remembering everything that

Caroline had told her about Bailey. Things hadn't changed that much, despite what Assistant Coach Carson wanted to think.

The two lapsed into silence then, and the assistant coach began flipping through the yearbook, turning the pages until she came to one that she paused on. Sam looked down at the spread and saw Missy's smiling face beaming out at her, an in-memoriam page devoted to the girl. Her hair was slicked back, wet from the pool, and she had her finger raised in a number one sign. There was a medal hanging around her neck, and something else. Something that Sam had to squint to see, that she leaned in really close to make sure she wasn't imagining.

"What's she wearing around her neck?" Sam asked, touching the necklace under her own shirt, feeling the tiny prongs of the laurel wreath crown.

"Her dad got it for her when she started high school," Assistant Coach Carson said. "It was a reminder of everything she was working toward. Victory."

"Do you know—" Sam broke off, not sure how to ask the question, not sure that it was even possible. "Do you know what happened to it?"

Assistant Coach Carson shook her head, shrugging. "It's kind of like the one you have," she said, as if only now remembering. She and Jenna had both stared a little too long at it during the last dual meet. "Where did you say you got yours?"

But before Sam could respond, Caroline burst into the

classroom, shouting like there was a fire. Like someone had died.

"Sam! I've been looking everywhere for you!" Caroline said. There was a rawness in her voice, something wild and barely contained. Her curly hair was a mess, the strands tangled together, falling in her face. Which made Sam start to panic.

"What's wrong?" Sam demanded, holding her breath, expecting the worst.

"I can't—" Caroline paused as she snuck a look at Assistant Coach Carson, realizing they weren't alone.

"Is everything okay?" The assistant coach got up from her desk, worry etched into her furrowed brow. "Do I need to call the nurse? Or the principal?"

"No! It's fine." Caroline rushed to get it out. "I just—can I borrow Sam for a minute? I really need her help with something. A school project."

Sam knew this was a lie, but she didn't wait for permission. She leapt out of her seat and ran to Caroline. She wrapped her hand around the girl's fingers and let her pull her out of the room. Let her lead her through the hallways at breakneck speed. They rushed past teachers and bumped into classmates. They slid across recently mopped floors and jumped over full backpacks. They didn't slow down or stop for a break or say a single word until Caroline suddenly came up short, winded, gasping and bent over for breath.

"What is it?" Sam pleaded. "What's wrong?"

She had no idea what was going on. And that not-knowing was killing her.

Eventually, Caroline managed to catch her breath. Managed to get three words out. "He's in there." She tipped her head toward the closed door in front of them, and Sam tentatively moved past her, nudging it open, preparing for the worst.

As she entered the storage closet, the first thing she heard was crying. But they weren't normal tears. They were heaving sobs. Guttural. Heart-wrenching.

She edged deeper into the room, moving around the shelving units, ignoring the stacks of textbooks and journals. She followed the wails until she found him there, curled up in a ball on the floor. Duncan. Only Sam didn't recognize him at first. She wasn't sure it was even him. Because instead of his usual, immaculately styled hair, there was nothing but skin, the red of fresh razor burn.

"Who—who did this to you?" Sam choked on the question, horrified at what had happened to her friend, unable to process it.

"It was—" Duncan sniffed, his fingers rubbing the rawness of his head, his hair shaved down, probably shorter than it'd been since he was a newborn. "It was Clark. And the rest of the team."

And in that terrible moment, something broke inside Sam.

Rage flooded through her, filling every inch of her body with an uncontrollable fury. This time, Clark had gone too far.

"He's not going to get away with this," Sam hissed. And then, before Duncan or Caroline could stop her, she launched herself into the hallway, anger blinding her, vengeance calling her name.

CHAPTER
TWENTY-TWO

The boys' locker room door slammed against the wall as Sam threw it open and barreled inside. She didn't care that she wasn't allowed in there, that she might stumble on the boys half-dressed, just out of the shower. She'd seen enough guys in Speedos over the years to not flinch when they had a little extra skin showing.

The place seemed empty, though, abandoned except for one swim bag sitting on the benches, Clark's name stitched on it in black thread along with the Wentworth High School *W*. Sam scanned the room, searching for him. For evidence, too. The electric razor was still out, lying on the counter under the mirrors, and there was a pile of hair in the sink, a collection of smooth blond locks that could only be Duncan's. Sam picked up some of the strands, weighing them, letting them drop through her fingers like snowfall.

Why would they do this to Duncan? Sam closed her eyes and imagined the fight he must have put up. How he would have shouted and bucked. How he would have protected himself at all costs. She could hear the electric razor's buzzing, an angry swarm of bees coming closer, their stingers set to bite into his scalp, to shave his head clean. How many boys would it have taken to hold him down? To keep him still while they took the clippers to his hair? How long had he struggled until he'd given in? Until he'd accepted their cruelty?

Sam snatched the razor off the counter and hurled it across the room, happy when it hit the wall, when it shattered into pieces, the plastic and metal flying in every direction. Duncan was a saint, and they were all monsters. Clark and the rest of them.

Make them pay.

Sam jerked her head to the side as she heard the showers turn off. She'd been so angry when she'd barged in that she hadn't even noticed they were on. But this was her chance. She could put Clark in his place, make him feel the hurt and pain he'd inflicted on Duncan. And then maybe he'd understand. Maybe he'd stop. Maybe he'd leave Duncan alone.

Not knowing exactly what she planned to do, Sam tiptoed toward the showers. She hid in the steam, letting the mist cover her completely, waiting for Clark to walk past her so that she could catch him off guard, could jump out and scare him.

Around her, the residual warmth of the shower turned

unnaturally cold. The water seeped into her clothes and she started to shiver. She crossed her arms over her chest and tried to hold on to her body heat, but before she knew it, her teeth were chattering. The water molecules clung to her hair. To the backs of her arms. To her face and neck. They collected and formed drops that slid down her body, like fingers tickling her flesh. She shivered again as a chill ran through her, as a hand fell on her shoulder, a presence gathering behind her. She spotted Clark's shadow moving through the mist, and it was as if someone pushed her forward, sent her careening toward him, a head-on collision.

"What are you doing in here?" Clark shouted, jumping as Sam materialized behind him. He'd already toweled off and pulled on a pair of athletic shorts, but he was still damp from his shower, dewdrops glittering on his skin.

Sam's first instinct was to reach back and punch him, but she held off, her hands clenched into fists at her sides. "Why'd you do that to Duncan?" she demanded, her body twitching, her fury barely contained.

"Duncan?" Clark barely seemed to register the name, which only made Sam madder. "Don't you have better things to worry about?"

"Duncan is my friend," Sam shot back, poking a finger into Clark's broad chest, though it did little to move him. "And you've been torturing him all season."

"Oh, come on. We're all just having fun. Some teasing. It's

what boys do." Clark chuckled as if it truly was nothing, as if Duncan had been in on the joke all year long instead of the butt of it.

"And shaving his head?" Sam wasn't backing down. "That's just a funny prank to you?"

"Relax." Clark seemed annoyed now, his easygoing demeanor falling away. "He had to match the rest of the team, didn't he? We all got them this morning. After practice."

He gestured to his own head, to his crisp buzz cut. But that was the haircut he always had. It was no different from any other day.

"You forced it on him." Sam didn't understand why he couldn't see how wrong that was. Why he refused to admit it. "You held him down and buzzed him bald."

Clark only looked at her with a dumbfounded grin on his face, a little boy knowing he'd done wrong and knowing that he'd get away with it.

"You're a monster," Sam hissed, seething now. "All of you are. And I hope you get what's coming to you." She whirled around to leave, but as she did, the locker room lights flickered, flipping on and then off and then on again. It startled Clark, and he took a few steps toward the shower as if he'd seen something in there.

"Very funny," Clark said, though he didn't sound amused. He turned around to face Sam and glowered down at her. He was done entertaining her. "This is the boys' locker room, so I think it's time for you to go."

Sam meant to sneer back at him, but the lights suddenly shut off again, throwing the whole room into shadow. A chill prickled up Sam's neck and she shivered. She blew a cold breath from her lungs, watched it fog right in front of her face. And then the light snapped back on. But this time, they weren't alone.

A figure stood in the showers, its outline captured in the mist left over from the hot spray. It shimmered in the light, and it took Sam a few seconds to recognize the bloated face. To place the shark-sharp teeth and gnarled hands. The scraggly, wet hair.

Sam yelped and held up a hand, pointing because she couldn't speak, because she needed to warn Clark about the actual monster looming behind him.

Too late.

Clark turned to look. He turned to meet Missy face-to-face. Her fingers darted toward him and dug into his mouth. Her arms turned to water, choking him, filling his lungs, drowning him where he stood. He gargled and jerked, his body convulsing as it bucked for air, as his eyes took one look at this demon and rolled into the back of his head. His legs collapsed underneath him and he plummeted to the floor, smashing his head against the tiles, cracking the porcelain.

Sam snapped into action.

She leapt forward, screaming, sobbing, reaching for Clark and praying it wasn't too late. She grabbed the towel he'd had around his shoulders and hurled it at Missy, and the spirit, mercifully, dissolved on contact, putrid water splashing against the floor, flooding the space. Sam ignored it, though, and shouted for help. She hovered over Clark's body and checked for breathing. For a pulse. She positioned her hands above his chest and started pumping, trying to expel the water from his lungs.

The doors to the boys' locker room flung open.

"What happened!" Caroline cried as she slid into the locker room.

She must have been looking for Sam since she'd abruptly left the storage closet, must have known who she was looking for.

"He's not breathing," Sam yelled back as she kept up the compressions, as her arms worked up and down on Clark's chest, one after the other after the other. She was losing him. She could feel his skin growing cold underneath her touch. "Not you, too."

Tears trickled down her cheeks and she poured all that emotion into resuscitating him, into bringing him back. She forced her hands down and finally he jerked underneath her. He sat up suddenly, a bilge of water spraying out of his mouth as he hacked up everything that Missy had forced down his lungs. He took in a shuddering breath and looked straight into Sam's eyes. A trail of blood leaked from his nose, and she couldn't tell if he was grateful to her or scared of her. Before she could ask, his eyes clouded over and he collapsed onto the floor, his chest rising as he lay there, alive but unconscious.

Sam fell back, her fingers pushing the hair out of her face, sliding across the sweat that had slid down from her forehead. She pulled them away and saw the red stains there. A bloody nose to match Clark's. It trickled onto the floor, mixing with the water, swirling around her. Her pulse pounded in her ears, but through that fog Sam could hear Caroline on the phone calling for an ambulance, getting her brother the help that he needed.

Sam was in shock. Missy had answered her unconscious call. Had come when she was furious. When she'd wanted so desperately to protect Duncan. To make Clark pay.

It was her fault. Her anger had put Clark in the hospital. It had almost killed him. She was dangerous. How could she say she was any better than Bailey?

CHAPTER
TWENTY-THREE

The locker room swam around Sam, the scene lit in shadowy blues and grays, everything moving in slow motion. Around her, the girls got ready, peeling off their swim caps and grabbing towels for the shower. Their voices bubbled up and spilled over, churning in the background, the soundtrack of camaraderie, of a team. But Sam wasn't a part of that. She was an outsider in their ranks. Adrift. Alone.

Not wanting to think about it, Sam crossed the room and headed to her locker. She was still dripping from practice, running late. She felt a sense of déjà vu as she spun through her combination, as she opened her locker and the foul stench of fish heads hit her like a smack to the face.

She jolted back, the horror of all that blood, those sightless eyes, turning her stomach. A chorus of laughter erupted behind her, and Sam could feel the fingers pointing in her direction, the whispered insults flying behind her back. But this time, something was different. This time, instead of screaming and running away, Sam held her ground. She stayed to fight.

Rage coursed through her bloodstream as she whirled around, as she came face-to-face with Bailey, who had her phone up, ready to capture the cruel moment, so proud of herself and the prank she'd pulled.

Sam's hand shot out and she ripped the device from Bailey's grip. She squeezed and it crumpled in her hand, her grip crushing, stronger than was humanly possible. But she didn't stop to wonder why. She kept going, turning her anger into action. Into an attack. She shoved Bailey and the girl flew. She slammed into the lockers so hard that she left a dent in the metal. And then she crumpled to the floor, groaning, her hair a frizzled mess, tears streaming down her face, blood dripping from the corner of her mouth.

The rest of the girls screamed and scattered, moving out of Sam's way, cowering in corners and underneath benches. A few even ran for the door. It was pandemonium, but it didn't bother Sam. Calmly, she made her way to Bailey. She reached down and grabbed the girl by the neck. She lifted her up like it was nothing, holding her inches above the ground. Her nails dug into the girl's flesh, forced a scream out of her. And as Bailey opened her mouth, she started to sputter, to choke and gag. Sam looked closer and was astonished to see the water seeping from her own hand, trickling past Bailey's lips, clawing its way down her throat and into her lungs.

As Bailey begged for mercy, Sam's gaze darted to the locker room mirror, to her profile reflected in it. And she froze, her heart drumming in her chest. She took in her demonic eyes, the bloodred irises. She faltered as she opened her mouth and a row of shark teeth flashed back at her. Her grip loosened and Bailey sagged to the floor, coughing, pathetic, halfway to dead. Sam backed away, horrified at what she saw. At what she'd done. At what she had become.

They'll never bother us again.

Gasping, Sam jerked upright in bed. She wheezed and panted, struggling to catch her breath as she tried to shake off the nightmare. Remembering what she'd dreamed, she scrambled to her feet and raced to the mirror. There were dark purple rings under both eyes, souvenirs from a few sleepless nights, but they were their normal brown. No razor-sharp teeth either.

She sighed, running her hand through her hair, pinching her cheeks to get some of the color back in them. She looked down at her palms, remembering how it had felt to have Bailey's throat in her grip, to wield that kind of power, and she shuddered.

Clark could have died. Paige had. It was clearer than ever what Missy wanted with Sam, but she refused to go along with the spirit's plan. She wouldn't let Missy feed on her anger, wouldn't let her enact her revenge. So many people had already gotten hurt. She couldn't add to that tally. She couldn't let Missy win. She'd just have to stay as far away from the water as she could. No going back to the pool. No swimming. It was the only way she could hope to keep everyone safe.

Sam stared herself down in the mirror, mouthing the words, making a promise. She noticed her necklace dangling against her chest, the laurel wreath charm glittering, warm to the touch. She ripped it over her head and threw it across the room. She watched as it thunked against the wall and bounced onto the floor. But it still seemed to pulse. Still called to her. Sam closed her eyes and was barely able to swallow her wail, barely able to keep it all together.

"Everything all right in here?" There was a knock at the bedroom door, and then Sam's dad poked his head inside. "What was all that noise?"

Her dad looked at her and then at the carpet, noticing the necklace lying there, discarded. He wavered for a moment and then took a step into the room, bending to pick it up. He studied it, his fingers massaging the two charms, going over their grooves. Then his fist closed. Squeezed tight. He turned to Sam. "I think it's time that we talked."

"Haven't we already done that?" Sam groaned, not wanting to get into it with him again. She didn't have the patience. She didn't think she could handle more of his disappointment, not with everything else weighing on her.

"It's different this time. I promise." Sam's dad held up a hand as if he was taking an oath. "I'm here to listen. To understand how you're feeling."

"Did Mom put you up to this?" Sam eyed him, unsure of whether she should trust what he was saying.

"She gave me some advice," her dad admitted. "But this is all me. It's something I wanted to do. For you."

Sam grimaced even as she nodded, moving over to sit in the middle of the bed. Better to get it over with so that he'd leave her alone.

"What do you want to talk about?" Sam asked, getting right to the point. "The fact that you think I should be swimming again?"

Her dad winced, the jab finding its mark. But he shook it off. Came back for more. "I guess I kind of deserve that," he said, his chin dipping in apology. "Your mom, she made me realize that I'd never stopped and checked in with you. Throughout all your training—the practices and dual meets and championship races—I'd never asked if you were having fun. If I was putting too much pressure on you. If you actually *wanted* to keep going."

Sam remained silent. Because it was true. He'd never asked. But that wasn't completely fair. She hadn't given him a hint that she was tired of it or wasn't enjoying herself. She never let on that she felt overwhelmed. They'd been in it together. She'd pushed just as hard as he had.

"So, that's what I'm here to do," her dad went on, filling the silence. "I want to know, are you burned out? Do you really want to quit swimming? Because if you do, that's fine. I understand. We can do that."

Sam didn't answer. But not because she was upset or annoyed. As she thought over her dad's question, she realized that she didn't know what to say. At least, not yet.

"I probably never told you this, but I went through the same thing in high school. I didn't play football my sophomore year."

"You didn't?" This shocked Sam and she readjusted her position on the bed so that she could see her dad better, so that she could witness the way his forehead creased as he spoke, as he remembered.

"I was going through a rough patch. I'd plateaued in the weight room. I wasn't meshing with my quarterback. I wasn't good enough to start on the varsity squad. I was miserable every second I was out on that field. So, I quit. Gave it all up."

Sam couldn't believe it. Her dad had loved football. He'd only stopped playing because he got hurt. It somehow changed everything she thought she knew about him.

"But you started playing again, right?" Sam asked, needing all the details.

"I did," her dad replied. "And that time away was what made me realize how much I loved the sport. How much I thrived on the competition. It's what pushed me to get back on the team, and work my butt off until I earned that varsity spot and a scholarship to play in college."

Sam frowned, her dad's story taking a sudden turn in the

direction of a pep talk, a get-back-out-there-and-do-your-best speech.

"I guess what I'm trying to say," her dad jumped in, realizing he was losing his audience, that he had done a poor job of making his point, "is that you need to figure out the reason why you swim. If you can answer that, then you'll know if you want to keep going or if you're ready to quit."

"I swim because I'm really good at it," Sam replied, as if it were a given. "Because I win."

Her dad chuckled, and this surprised Sam.

"What? It's true, isn't it?"

"It's true," her dad agreed, pulling himself together. "But do you remember what you said to me the very first time you won a race?"

Sam shook her head. She didn't have a clue. She didn't even know the first time she'd won. How old had she been? Six? Or seven?

"You came running up to me with that blue ribbon in your hand and you said, 'Daddy, Daddy, Daddy, look what I got. Wouldn't Kasey be so proud?'" He opened his palm then and the seashell charm caught the light. It winked at her, as if it had a secret to share.

"I still miss her sometimes," Sam whispered, words failing her suddenly. "I think about why I'm somehow still here when she's not."

She'd never told her dad how she truly felt. She'd always

put on a strong front. But there was a power in letting go now. A sense of lightening, like an anchor had been loosened from around her ankle. She could float back up to the surface and let go of that big breath she'd been holding on to for years.

"It was an accident, sweetheart," her dad said, his voice low and soothing. "A terrible thing that I wish had never happened. But I know she'd be on your side. She'd be right at the end of your lane cheering you on. She would be proud of who you've become. Both in the water and out of it."

Sam sniffed, tears trickling out of the corners of her eyes. She tried to blink them away, but they wouldn't stop. They kept coming.

"Take your time and think about it," her dad said, holding the necklace out for her to take. "And know that the decision you make right now, today, it doesn't have to be your decision forever. You can change your mind. The pool will always be there for you if you decide it's where you want to be."

Sam gulped, and with a shaking hand, she reached out and took the necklace. Then she wrapped her arms around her dad's neck and she hugged him, squeezing him tight. "Thank you," she whispered. And that was enough. It was all she needed to say to make him understand.

"It sounds like someone's here to see you," Sam's dad said as they pulled out of their embrace, his ears perking up when another knock came at the front door. "Is it okay if I let them in?"

Sam rubbed her eyes with the backs of her hands and

nodded. Her dad patted her arm and then rose from the bed, only groaning a little as his leg stiffened and his knee popped. Then he made his way out of the room, his usual shuffling step trailing him down the hallway. Sam heard the front door open, and a few moments later Caroline and Duncan burst into sight, throwing themselves onto her bed.

"Are you all right?" Caroline mumbled, her voice muffled as she pressed her face into Sam's shoulder.

"I'm okay," Sam replied as she pulled herself free, trying not to laugh at the affection, at how good it made her feel. "How's Clark?"

This was what she really needed to know, what had been eating at her for the last couple of days.

Caroline provided an update. "He's still in the hospital. He's awake, though. They have him on a respirator, but he's going to be fine."

"I'm sorry," Sam whispered, relief breaking over her even as the guilt of what had happened sat heavily on her heart. "I didn't mean to—"

"You didn't do anything," Caroline insisted. "It was out of your control. It was Missy."

Sam fell quiet. She didn't know how to tell them that her anger had summoned the girl's spirit. That her fury had set Missy on Clark.

"And you were the one who rescued him," Caroline went on. "The CPR you did—it saved his life."

Sam swallowed, uncomfortable still, not wanting to take any credit. Not thinking that she deserved it.

"You had us worried there," Duncan said. "The way you went completely off the grid. We didn't know what happened to you."

And it was true. After the paramedics had carted Clark away, Sam had run home. She'd switched off her phone and gone into a black hole. She hadn't checked social media or anything. She'd wanted to disappear, hadn't wanted to face anyone.

"How's your hair?" Sam asked, noticing that Duncan had on a beanie.

"It'll grow back." He winced as he scratched his head and pulled the knit cap down low to his eyebrows. "And until then, I have some time to figure out which hat fits my head shape best."

Sam sputtered, trying not to laugh. She didn't know how Duncan could get over an incident like that so quickly. How he could move on from it. But maybe he was just putting on a brave face. Making the most out of a poor situation. It wasn't like he could do anything about it now.

"Once my brother gets out of the hospital, I'm going to kill him," Caroline muttered. "I still can't believe he—"

"I think he's suffered enough." Duncan stopped her, signaling that he'd had enough of the conversation.

"Well," Caroline spitballed, glancing around their circle, looking at each of them in turn. "What now?"

And here was the opening Sam needed. She hadn't had much time to think it through, but her dad had reminded her of what she'd been missing these last couple of months. He'd reminded her of why she swam. It was time to stop wallowing. It was time to get up and do something. She had the seeds of a plan, but she needed help to pull it off.

Holding the necklace in the palm of her hand, Sam said a little prayer to Kasey. She focused on the girl's seashell, on her memory, on what had gotten Sam so excited to swim back when she was six.

"Now we banish a ghost."

As Sam filled her friends in on everything that had happened—her visions of the past and Missy's voice in her head, the way the girl's spirit had tried to take control of her body, how Jenna and Assistant Coach Carson and the necklace she'd found at the bottom of the graveyard pool were all connected—her plan began to come into shape. It started to solidify. She wasn't sure it would work, but she had to try. For Caroline and Duncan and herself. For Kasey. She couldn't give up without a fight.

CHAPTER
TWENTY-FOUR

The next day at school, the hours dragged by, making Sam feel like she'd never get to the end of it. But when the last bell finally did ring, she burst out of her seat and rushed into the hallway. She made straight for her locker, for the supplies she'd carefully gathered the night before.

Pulling her backpack tight around her shoulders, Sam paused. She thought about what she was about to attempt, the fact that there was no guarantee that it would work. It wasn't science. She hadn't found a handy manual online for banishing evil spirits or anything. But she did have a better idea of what Missy wanted, what was keeping her from passing on. And she thought that she could give the girl peace. At least, she hoped that she could help her find rest.

"Everything ready?" Duncan asked as he came up behind Sam. He had on a beret today, the black fabric slouching in an artful swoop. It suited him. It brought out the angles of his jawline.

"Almost," Sam said as she closed her locker. She tugged on her backpack straps, nerves getting the best of her. This wasn't like a race. She couldn't just swallow the jitters down. She couldn't ignore them. "Waiting on confirmation from Caroline. Then we're a go."

Duncan bit his bottom lip and scratched at his head absently. He moved to lean against the lockers, and Sam was relieved to see him tapping his foot, anxious, too. At least her fear was legitimate. She wasn't the only one who felt it.

They stood there next to each other, the halls emptying around them, their classmates packing up and heading home. A part of Sam wished she could do the same. Wished she could ignore everything and leave it for someone else to handle. But she'd already decided. She had to face this. *She* had the connection with Missy. She was the only person who could stop her.

"I'm glad I ran into you," a voice said out of nowhere. She had to snap out of her daze to realize that it was Assistant Coach Carson standing in front of her, an expectant look on her face. "We didn't get a chance to finish our conversation from the other day."

Sam hesitated, unsure of what to say. But she couldn't exactly turn away from her teacher, her former coach, so she swallowed, the moisture wetting her dry mouth, and she replied.

"Good to see you, too." Sam's voice wavered, nervousness

spilling over. But Assistant Coach Carson didn't seem to notice as she kept right on with the point she'd wanted to make.

"Have you had any second thoughts about quitting the team? I know Coach Hendricks would love to have you back," Assistant Coach Carson said. "And we can work on *anything* that might have been bothering you. That might have gotten in the way of your training."

The assistant coach's emphasis told Sam that the woman had actually listened to her. That she had looked into what had been going on. She might not have found out the full extent of what Clark and Bailey had pulled, but she knew that something had gone down. And she was willing to make an effort to change it. To make things better.

"Talking to you about Missy," the assistant coach continued because Sam hadn't said anything. "It reminded me of one of the reasons why I became a teacher. It was one of the things that I'd hoped to change from when I was in school." She took a deep breath, her gaze shifting between Sam and Duncan. And then she laid it out there plain and simple. "Missy was my best friend in high school, and she had to put up with some pretty merciless bullying. No one seemed willing to help her back then. But I'm going to put an end to it now. I don't care what Coach Hendricks or the principal or the parents say. I want to make sure the team is a safe space. I want *everyone* to feel welcome."

It was exactly what Sam had wanted to hear, and she could

feel Duncan perking up next to her. She didn't know if Assistant Coach Carson's plan would work, if it would effect any real change, but at least she was acknowledging what had been going on. At least she planned to try to make it better. It was something. It was a start.

"That sounds good," Sam murmured. "It sounds great, actually. I really appreciate it."

"I hope you'll reconsider," Assistant Coach Carson said with an earnestness that set hooks in Sam's core, that made her not want to tell this woman no. "I hope you'll come back to the team. I would hate it if a few bullies forced you out of the pool. And I wouldn't be able to live with myself if you end up quitting because no one stepped in to protect you."

Sam stood there frozen, at a loss for words. She'd never had a coach talk to her this way. Never had an adult speak so honestly to her.

"I'll think about it," Sam eventually stammered.

And she was going to say more, but at that exact moment Caroline came barging around the corner, huffing like she'd run the length of the school to get to them. She spotted Assistant Coach Carson and came up short, unsure of whether she should interrupt, unsure if the woman would think they were losing it if she found out what they were attempting. Or worse, if she'd try to stop them. So instead of coming over, she shot Sam a thumbs-up and waved for her to follow.

"Um—" Sam sputtered, looking back and forth between

the coach and Caroline. "Sorry, but I've got to go. There's something I need to take care of." And Sam didn't know why she felt the need to add this, but as she grabbed Duncan's arm and pulled him away toward Caroline, she gave her assistant coach a parting compliment, something she hoped the woman would hold on to. "Missy would be proud of what you're doing. She'd be glad to know that you still think of her. And that you remember."

A smile bloomed on Assistant Coach Carson's lips, and Sam just managed to catch it as she whipped around the corner.

"You sure you're ready for this?" Caroline asked, picking on the same question as Duncan.

And this time, Sam didn't hesitate. The nerves had settled in her stomach. Had morphed into determination. "Let's do this."

The three of them charged forward, heading back to the pool. Back to where Missy was waiting for them.

CHAPTER
TWENTY-FIVE

The door creaked open as they entered the pool, the noise echoing up and off the high ceiling, making a cavern of the room. They tiptoed inside as if they were in a haunted house, every single one of them on high alert, ready for a jump scare. A lone figure churned in the lanes, throwing up white water as they swam along. At first, Sam thought it was Missy, her ghostly avatar doing laps. But then she recognized the stroke. The breathing pattern. The cap with the girl's last name stenciled on it.

Bailey.

Sam watched as she came into the wall and flipped, her strokes surer than they'd been before, her underwater dolphin kicks more powerful. So this was how she'd gotten better. This was how she'd caught up. Though she despised her, Sam was impressed by Bailey's dedication. She even admired it.

"Can we still do the séance with her in the pool?" Caroline asked, her forehead scrunching up in concern.

Sam tore her eyes away from the water and scanned the deck, as if she'd find an answer there. "I don't know."

Frustration and doubt flooded through her brain, washing away any previous confidence that she'd had. As if things hadn't been uncertain enough before, now she had to contend with this new wrinkle, a variable that could throw everything off. They were two seconds into her plan and already it was going awry.

Originally, her idea had been to summon Missy's spirit just like they had at the graveyard pool, by using Caroline's old Ouija board. Only this time when Missy answered the call, Sam would be ready. She'd be able to talk to her. She'd reason with her. Settle her down. And maybe that would help set her spirit at rest.

At least, that had been her hope. But now she didn't know if the summoning would even work. And if it did, would Sam be able to control Missy? Or would her spirit go after Bailey like it had Paige and Clark?

A door banged open and Sam jumped. But it was only Coach Hendricks emerging from his office, clipboard in hand, his stopwatch looped around his neck.

"Change your mind about quitting the team?" he asked brightly when he spotted her, completely missing the way her jaw had locked up, the tension that had coiled into her shoulders. "I knew you couldn't stay away for long. You like winning too much. You're too talented. I'm happy to add you into Bailey's after-school routine. She's come a long way in the past few weeks with her two-a-day practices. She's been training her butt off. Motivated by catching up to you, I think. Nothing like a little competition to push the best out of someone."

He said it like it was nothing. Like Bailey hadn't been gunning for Sam since day one, both in the pool and in the locker room. Like she hadn't resorted to low blows, to psychological warfare, to win-at-all-costs tactics.

"No—um—I didn't." Sam balked, drawing back, finally seeing Coach Hendricks for who he truly was. "We were actually—"

But what could she say? He wouldn't believe her if she told him why they were there. And now that she thought about it, she realized that he'd only ever cared about her when she was in the pool. He'd congratulated her on her splits and turnover rate and technique. He'd encouraged her when she'd finished in first place with good times. But he'd also stoked that rivalry between her and Bailey. He'd forced them into a fight by putting them in the same event, switching their lane assignments.

And, Sam now realized, he'd done it on purpose. He'd meant to drive a wedge between them. He'd looked the other way when Bailey had bullied her. He'd purposely put them up against each other. Was that really his brand of coaching? His strategy for motivation?

Sam wanted to spit. She wanted to show him what she really thought. He only cared about winning. About making himself look good. He was a selfish man and a bad coach.

Sam turned to face him then. "Tell me what really happened to Missy." She startled herself as the demand came out of her mouth. This hadn't been part of her plan, but he *had* been in that vision. He had stood by while Jenna badmouthed Missy. While she convinced the boys to cannonball in on top of her. Had he been trying to pit the two girls against each other, too? Was the rivalry between Bailey and Sam a carbon copy of what he'd set up for Missy and Jenna?

"Who?" Coach Hendricks asked, but Sam wasn't buying it.

"Missy Caplin," Sam said, using the girl's full name. "And don't act like you don't remember. You know what really happened to her."

The head coach's eyes shifted. He was suddenly very uncomfortable. Antsy like Sam had never seen him before.

"All the details were in the police report," he mumbled, the canned response coming out like he was a robot. "It was in the papers, too. An accidental drowning. Just like Paige's. That's all there was to it. A horrible tragedy."

"Are you sure about that?" A vein throbbed in Sam's neck as her jaw clenched. That tidal wave of anger was rising up in her again, threatening to take over, to capsize all her plans. "Tell me the truth."

A pause stretched between them, the two locked in a

staring contest. Coach Hendricks wasn't playing nice anymore. He'd turned serious. Calculating. His exterior stony. "You better watch the way you speak to me."

There was danger in Coach Hendricks's voice, a warning not to push him too far. But Sam was tired of the lies. She needed answers. And so did Missy.

"What's going on?"

The tension in the air snapped as Jenna Miller appeared in the door. She smacked on a piece of gum while she took them all in, confusion mixing with curiosity.

"Jenna!" Caroline exclaimed, jumping into action and heading over to meet the woman. "I'm so glad you could make it."

"You said there was going to be some kind of get-well party for your brother?" Jenna frowned as she scanned the pool, realizing quickly that there was no one else there. "Am I early?"

Caroline shook her head and snagged Jenna's elbow, anchoring her in place, keeping her from leaving. Since Bailey and Clark were dating, Caroline had volunteered to lure Jenna there. They'd met a couple of times at holiday gatherings and family get-togethers, and Caroline had her number. A little white lie about her hospitalized brother and Jenna had agreed to meet them at the pool, where they'd planned to interrogate her about Missy. Now they had to make sure that it wasn't for nothing.

"What were you all talking about just now?" she asked. "I heard you mention Missy Caplin."

"You swam with her, didn't you?" Sam shifted her focus to Jenna. "Bailey said you two were teammates. *Best friends.*" Sam hit these last words hard, searching for a reaction, for a give-away in Jenna's response.

"We weren't very close," Jenna replied evenly. "We didn't really know each other that well."

"You hated her." They all spun around as Assistant Coach Carson joined their ranks, her fists clenched into tight balls as her body trembled. "You made her life hell."

Sam didn't know where the woman had come from, but she was glad for the backup, happy to have an adult on their side.

"I think you're misremembering," Jenna replied. "It was a long time ago. I was just a kid. It's understandable."

"Stop lying!" Sam's outburst brought everything to a stand-still. Even Bailey, in the pool, heard.

Sam's eyes tracked the girl as she coasted into the wall and held up, taking her goggles off to see what was happen-ing, why there were suddenly six people standing on the deck, yelling at each other. But as Bailey stopped, Sam noticed something else out there with her. Something churning and bubbling and growing in strength. Something violent, on the cusp of crashing over.

"Get out of the water!" Sam shouted as she raced to the edge of the pool and grabbed Bailey, yanking her up and out right as a wave crested. Right as it came crashing down and collided with the deck, throwing its spray all over them.

"What the—" Bailey shouted as the water drew back, as it sucked at her toes and tried to pull her in with it. But Sam had a firm grip on her arm. She wouldn't let Missy take her.

Before they could scramble to their feet and retreat to drier ground, a second wave tore through the pool and hit them. The force of it was stronger than the first. It threw Sam back, slamming her against the deck, knocking the breath out of her. Water seeped through her clothes and clung to her skin. It trickled up her nose, causing her whole head to smart, to sizzle with pain.

She blinked and her vision grew blurry. It shimmered like a mirage. And then, suddenly, Missy was standing there in front of her, her hair tucked under a cap, her Wentworth swimsuit bright and new and untorn. A necklace glittered around her neck, and Sam gasped as she realized where she was, as she understood that she was about to find out what had really happened to Missy on the day that she'd drowned.

CHAPTER
TWENTY-SIX

"Let's get going, ladies." Coach Hendricks's voice shocked Sam when it burst through the air, and she had to take a step back as she spotted him on the edge of the pool, looking mostly the same, just ten years younger.

A splash brought her attention back around, and she watched as Missy glided beneath the surface, as she kicked and pulled and broke out, her stroke long and easy, settling in for the warm-up. She sliced her way down the pool, swimming as naturally as a fish. She was one with the water, and Sam couldn't help but be a little mesmerized by her.

"Move it," Coach Hendricks interrupted, speaking to the rest of the girls, who were still loitering on the deck. "I don't care if it's cold. You're not going to catch up to Missy if you keep wasting time."

Sam spotted Jenna in their ranks. She clocked the way the

girl rolled her eyes, how she muttered under her breath. But before Sam could pick up anything she had said, Jenna fastened her goggles over her eyes and dove in, the rest of the team following her lead.

The practice went along smoothly after that, with Missy taking the lead and Jenna swimming in her wake. They didn't speak to each other in between sets. They barely acknowledged each other at all. It was like they had a silent, mutual understanding. But Sam could still sense the tension between them. She noticed how Missy's shoulders remained tight. How Jenna managed to splash water in her face almost every time she came into the wall. The girls chatted with Jenna but then ignored Missy altogether. They stuck out their tongues when Coach Hendricks praised her technique or challenged her to hit faster times than the rest of them. It was clear that there was a pecking order. That one of them was not welcome. But despite all that, Missy managed to keep her cool. She swam and hit her splits. She seemed unshakable.

"Let's finish up today with some time trials."

Everyone groaned as Coach Hendricks clicked his pen and tapped the point against his clipboard, clearly enjoying himself. Practice was almost over, and everyone was tired. A time trial forced them to compete, to show how they stacked up against one another. It was something that Sam excelled at, and she knew that Missy would, too.

As Coach Hendricks called out the first matchup, the

swimmers he named moved to the blocks. They took their marks and dove into the water, sprinting all out like it was an actual race. Coach Hendricks clocked their times as they came into the wall, shouting them out for everyone to hear while he jotted down notes before moving on to the next group. They went through this process four or five times until Missy and Jenna were the only two who hadn't gone.

"And for our last race . . ." Coach Hendricks drew it out as if there was a drumroll backing him. "We've got Missy and Jenna. Let's see if someone can unseat our champion."

He grinned at Jenna, but she seemed over it. Nonetheless, the two girls got up on the blocks, crouching low and launching forward when Coach Hendricks yelled go. They hit the pool at the same time, breaking through the surface, water flying as their arms spun and their feet kicked.

At first, Jenna kept pace with Missy. She matched her stroke for stroke. But when they flipped at the halfway point, Missy surged ahead. Jenna was no match for her. And as they sprinted into the last wall, pouring everything they had left into it, Missy finished more than two seconds in front.

"Come on, Jenna," Coach Hendricks yelled as she touched the wall and pulled off her goggles. He had his hands thrown up as if he didn't understand how she could have lost. "I know you can do better than that. You're embarrassing yourself, letting her beat you by a whole body length."

He shook his head and Jenna's grip tightened on the wall.

She glared over at Missy, her cheeks puffed out and red. Missy didn't meet her gaze, though. The girl kept her gaze straight ahead, most likely knowing from experience that ignoring Jenna was the best way to stay off her radar, to stay out of a fight.

"That's it for today," Coach Hendricks said, wrapping up practice. "Hit the showers. Eat a good breakfast. Make sure you get to bed early tonight. Tomorrow's going to be another hard one. We're building winners here. So, let's make sure we act like ones."

Sam watched as Missy pushed out of the water and sat on the edge of the pool. It looked like she was thinking over Coach Hendricks's words, reflecting on what it meant to be a champion. She had her necklace held out in front of her, the laurel wreath pinched between her fingers. Sam moved closer, curious, not wanting to miss anything.

One lane over, Jenna huffed as she got out of the pool. Sam's stomach clenched as Jenna's shadow fell across Missy's shoulders, as the girl glowered down at her rival.

"You think you're untouchable," she murmured, her voice seething with hatred. "You think you're better than the rest of us."

Missy turned and blinked up at Jenna, her fingers still holding the charm.

"Give me that."

And Sam gasped as Jenna snatched the necklace from

around Missy's throat, the clasp audibly snapping as it broke apart.

"Don't!" Missy cried, jumping to her feet. "My dad gave that to me."

"Well, I guess you'll be quick to go after it, then."

And without another word, Jenna launched the necklace into the pool, where it hit the water with a plop and sank straight to the bottom.

"Why'd you do that?" Missy shouted.

"Because I can," Jenna replied, drawing each word out, enjoying every syllable.

"You're such a—" But Missy didn't finish her sentence.

Jenna wasn't listening anyway. The girl wouldn't be moved. So, Missy did the only thing she could. She pressed her goggles back over her eyes and dove into the pool, drowning out Jenna's self-satisfied laughter as the water rushed in and filled her ears.

Sam was next to Missy now, the memory tying them together, moving through the water in slow motion. She found that she couldn't breathe. That she could only see the world in the same blue tint as Missy. Was this it, then? Was this when Missy drowned? Sam couldn't see how. But why else would Missy have brought her here?

A ringing filled Sam's ears as they dove deeper and the water pressure built. She followed along as Missy surveyed the bottom of the pool, scouring every corner for her necklace but coming up empty-handed. It was a small piece of jewelry, easy to lose and hard to find. As they drifted, Sam could feel her lungs growing tighter, the pain in her chest building.

Finally, on their third pass around the deep end, Missy seemed to spot something. She pointed and shot forward, a stream of bubbles escaping through her lips. She skimmed the bottom of the pool, her fingers dragging along the plastic, following the trail. And now Sam saw it, too. The thin body of a silver eel darting through the water, moving on the pool's invisible currents, heading straight for the drain.

With a jolt of panic, Missy swam after it. She reached out and grabbed for it right as it disappeared from sight. Sam thought Missy had lost it, but then she noticed a glimmer of metal, saw that Missy had managed to snag the end of the necklace's chain at the last second.

Relief broke over Sam. But then, quickly, it turned to fear. Because hadn't she found that same necklace in this very drain ten years later?

As if the memory had heard Sam's thought, Missy jerked back. Sam could see that the girl still had a hold on the necklace, but it must have hooked on something. Missy's arm strained as she tried over and over again to pull the thing free, but it wouldn't budge. She tried adjusting her angle, tried to get more leverage, tried pushing off with her legs, but nothing worked. And with each effort, Missy was losing oxygen. Was running out of time.

Sam felt the pressure building in her own head, felt her

lungs squeezing in on themselves, desperate, starving. Her pulse pounded in her ears, and she knew Missy must be feeling the same. Must have been light-headed, close to losing it. Sam looked at the girl and tried to urge her to the surface. She could dive back down and get the necklace after she'd taken a breath. But Missy kept at it, kept tugging two and three and then four more times.

Finally, she seemed to give up. She seemed to acknowledge that she could only last another thirty seconds or so underwater. She twisted to get her feet under her, to push off the bottom of the pool, but then she stopped. She wriggled the other way but came up short again. She tried repositioning her body, but no matter how she bent, she couldn't seem to move. She couldn't seem to get out of there. And suddenly, Sam felt a pain biting into her own flesh. It seared and was quickly followed by a wave of preternatural fear. Because Missy was stuck.

In all her attempts to yank the necklace free, the girl must have inadvertently gotten it looped around her wrist. And now, with her lungs shredded and screaming for air, she only had seconds to escape.

Frantic, Missy wrenched her arm back, using every muscle in her body. When that didn't work, she dug her fingernails under the edges of the drain and tried prying it open. As Missy strained to get free, Sam swam down to help her. But what could she do? Her hands passed right through Missy's arms. They wouldn't grab on to the drain cover. She couldn't do anything. She could only watch as Missy struggled. She could only count the tears as they leaked out of the girl's eyes and collected in the plastic cups of her goggles. She could only stand by and witness the last moments of Missy's life.

With her last surge of energy, Missy yanked her arm back, and then, finally, her wrist came free.

But it was already too late. Missy had pushed herself too far. Her thoughts had gone dark. Her pulse had slowed to an almost nonexistent beat. Her body lifted away from the drain and hung there in the in-between. And Sam could only watch as the unconscious girl floated in the depths, as the last bubbles of air trickled from her mouth.

It was terribly sad. A tragedy. And there was nothing at all that Sam could do to change it. She could only sit with Missy. Could only drift alongside the girl until the ringing in her ears grew unbearable, until the sound of the water pressure turned into the flatline beep of a heart monitor. Until Missy was officially gone. Drowned.

Then she screamed.

CHAPTER
TWENTY-SEVEN

Sam's scream echoed through the pool, bouncing off the walls, piercing through the black current that had dragged her under. She gasped and came back to life, her eyes opening wide, the cool air a balm for her aching lungs. She gulped breath after breath like it was water, her head spinning, her heart drumming, picking up speed as if it needed to remind itself that it hadn't stopped beating. A red line cut across her wrist, the wound where the necklace chain had bit into Missy's flesh. Into hers, too. Gingerly, Sam touched it, pulled back, still processing what had happened. Still stunned by the events she had witnessed.

Around her, a grim quiet had fallen. Everyone was looking in her direction, not understanding where she had gone or what she now knew.

"It was you," she murmured, her finger shaking as she pointed at Jenna. "And you."

She turned her accusation on Coach Hendricks.

"What are you talking about?" he countered, his arms snaking across his chest.

"You're the reason Missy drowned."

And while it had been an accident, Missy's necklace snagging and trapping her underwater, it had been Jenna's bullying that had led to it. It had been Coach Hendricks forcing the girls into competition, admonishing one while praising the other, overlooking the teasing and harassment, fostering an atmosphere of hate and rivalry and aggression on his team. They had both played a part in Missy's death. And they both needed to be held responsible.

"I wasn't a part of that," Coach Hendricks stuttered, putting his hands up, backing away from Sam. "Practice was over. I wasn't there."

"But you encouraged the rivalry," Sam spat out. "You wanted them at each other's throats because you thought it'd make them faster or something twisted like that. You were their coach. You should have stepped in and stopped it. You should have prevented it before it went too far."

Sam couldn't contain herself. Her fury radiated off her, hitting them all in waves. And behind her, the water responded. It churned and boiled. It lapped over the edge of the pool, reaching for Coach Hendricks as if responding to Sam's emotions, her need for revenge.

"What's happening?" Coach Hendricks stammered, his

eyes growing large as the water rolled over the side of the pool. "I'm getting out of here."

He turned to flee, but stream of water flowed just after him, forming a puddle of water under his feet. He slipped and slid. He stumbled for a few steps like he was walking on ice, and then he came crashing down, his head smacking against the deck, the sound of a bowling ball hitting solid concrete. He lay there, unmoving, his nose and mouth pressed into the ground. But the water wasn't done with him yet. Missy had other plans. The puddle shifted underneath him, rising to cover his face, to create a pool big enough for him to drown in.

"No!" Sam snapped out of her rage, the violence in that fall shocking her system, making her see straight again. She sprinted across the deck and grabbed Coach Hendricks's shoulders. She tried to twist him around, but it was like his face was suctioned to the ground. He wouldn't budge. The others gathered around, screaming as Sam kicked at the puddle, stomping on it, trying to disperse it, and finally he came free. She swung him around and leaned him up against a wall. He was still unconscious, but she could hear him breathing. She could feel his pulse. He was a dishonest, self-absorbed man, but he didn't deserve to die like that. No one did.

Drying her hands on her shirt, Sam spun around to face everyone. But whatever she was going to say died in her throat. Was replaced by someone's scream as a figure rose from the pool deck, as it materialized out of all the water that had spilled over.

And there she was, Missy, in the flesh, standing among them, her skin bloated and loose, hanging off her in patches. Her hair a ratty mess. Her razor-sharp teeth bared, glinting as her dead eyes scanned them all, searching for her next victim. Someone who needed to pay.

The moisture in the air froze solid, locking them all in place, preventing them from escaping, from running for their lives. They could only gawk and stare at the demon in their midst, at Missy's horrible, decaying form. Sam had never seen her so fully rendered. So real. She could smell the foul odor of standing water. Of rotting flesh. The chilly prickle of death crept up the back of her neck as the demon homed in on Jenna, studying her, her teeth bared. Sam wondered if she recognized the girl as her old tormentor. If she was here, finally, for her revenge.

Missy slid closer and Jenna trembled, her hand clutched tightly to her chest. The black beads on her bracelet sucked the light that tried to reflect off of them. Missy recoiled. She pulled back. Sam racked her brain and recalled what Jenna had said the first time they'd met, how she'd told Sam that the crystals on her bracelet were supposed to ward off evil spirits. But could that actually be true? Did they really work? Before Sam could think too much on it, Missy had shifted her focus. She'd decided on a new target.

"Watch out!" Sam cried, but it was too late. Bailey didn't have time to dive out of the way.

Missy surged forward, her hands wrapping around the girl's arms, turning to sheets of water that rushed across her skin, that made a necklace around her throat and squeezed. Bailey's cheeks paled, and her lips started to turn blue. She gasped, trying to breathe, choking on the nothing that got through, and Missy took the opening, her water pouring into Bailey's mouth, causing her to convulse, to shake uncontrollably,

"Your bracelet," Sam shouted as she raced forward, frantically gesturing at a stunned Jenna, willing her to understand, to get that she could save her sister. "Give it to me."

Her words broke through and Jenna scratched at her arm as she yanked the string of black beads from her wrist. Sam grabbed them and pressed them into Bailey's palms, using her own hands to guide Bailey to her neck, to the water that was streaming into her open mouth.

A hiss tore through the air as steam rose from the pool deck. From Bailey. Her body gave a shudder and then she threw up, exorcising the demon in one violent upheaval. She fell to her knees, her shoulders heaving as she took great, desperate gulps. Slowly, the color returned to her face and her eyes came back into focus. She turned to Sam and gave her a nod, issuing her thanks.

But it wasn't over yet. Missy was still there with them,

water filtering across the pool deck, a tide rising, regrouping, ready to launch another attack.

"Everybody, take one."

And before Sam could worry that something might go wrong, she snapped the bracelet's thin metal chain. The black tourmaline beads came loose in her hands. She divided them up, handing one to Caroline and Duncan and Assistant Coach Carson. Dropping one in Bailey's and Jenna's open hands. She even made sure the unconscious Coach Hendricks had one tucked into his shirt, and then she kept the last for herself, thankful that they had just enough.

"Don't lose these," she commanded. "They're the only thing standing between us and her."

Everyone nodded, immediately understanding the importance of these talismans.

"Now help me push her back." Sam held her bead out in front of her. She worried that the charms might not hold as much power broken up like this, but if they all combined their efforts, then maybe it would be enough.

Caroline joined her first. And then Duncan was at her side. It didn't take long for Assistant Coach Carson, Jenna, and Bailey to fall in line. They had Missy surrounded, and they used that power to push her up against the pool. To make sure that she had nowhere else to go but back into the water.

With a splash, the demon disappeared. But standing on the edge of the pool, Sam could still sense Missy's movements below, could spot the eddies and ripples of her wake as she darted through the deep end. She was contained, but not gone.

"What is happening?" Bailey sobbed, breaking down into a frantic fit. "What is that thing? And why did it try to kill me?"

"There's no time to explain," Sam shot back. "Just trust me, it's bad."

"Was that Missy?" Jenna murmured, a haunted look in her eye. "Was that her ghost? Did I do that to her?"

Sam only nodded, barely registering the confession that the shock of seeing Missy had shaken out of the woman.

"I didn't know," Jenna mumbled. "I didn't mean to—"

"You can deal with your guilt later," Assistant Coach Carson snapped. "First we need to figure out how to help her."

The group turned to Sam, expecting an answer, a course of action. She tugged on the straps of her backpack and tried to think straight. Tried to find the words to explain what she needed them to do. She was still guessing on all of this, but what other choice did they have?

"I need to talk to her," Sam said. "I need to get her to listen. I know what she's been through. I know how she feels. She's angry and hurting, but I think I can get through."

Sam loosened her grip on her backpack and pulled it off. She set it on the deck and started rummaging through it. She ignored the Ouija board. She didn't need any help summoning Missy now that she was already there. But she did need help containing her. Keeping her at bay long enough so that she could speak to her, reason with her, quell her anger and hopefully give her peace.

Finding what she needed, Sam fished her hand out of her backpack and produced the five-pound bag of salt she'd brought along for emergencies.

"We need to sprinkle this around the edge of the pool," she explained. "We have to encircle the whole thing. It'll help protect us, create a barrier that Missy can't break through. The salt should keep her at bay while I try to reason with her."

Everyone nodded, understanding the instructions and not asking any follow-up questions. Missy's appearance had already stretched the scope of their imaginations, so they didn't stop to worry about the danger they were putting themselves in as they bent over and took giant handfuls of the salt.

"Make sure you don't leave any gaps," Sam insisted. "And don't touch the water. Don't give Missy an opportunity to grab you."

Sam looked past them at the pool, gulping as the water churned, as she spotted a ghostly figure circling, cutting a deadly path through the deep end.

"If she pulls any of us in, we won't stand a chance. So be careful."

This went without saying, but Sam did anyway. She was the only one who'd actually been in the pool with Missy. The only one who understood how helpless a situation it was. She'd survived before, but that didn't guarantee that Missy would let her escape again. She seemed angry enough to attack anyone within reach. Anyone trying to stand in the way of her revenge.

"Let's do this," Caroline muttered, and they all set to the task.

It took longer to spread the salt than Sam had imagined. The perimeter of the pool was large—almost seventy-five yards—and they had to lay it on thick. If there was even a millimeter of a break, Missy would be able to slip through. But they could only hold so much salt at one time. They kept having to return to the bag and refill their fists. Eventually they realized that they could carry more per trip if they used their shirts, but it was a grinding process nonetheless, their hands growing raw and chapped, their nerves fraying as Missy batted against their efforts, as she sent wave after wave in their direction, spilling over the edge of the pool, trying to catch them unawares. Thankfully, they managed to retreat each time, to harness their black tourmaline beads, to continue their work slowly and methodically.

Like that, they were able to make their way around the pool. They were almost done when Sam's fingernails scraped the bottom of the bag, when she realized they were out of salt. She glanced over at Caroline and saw that they only had a small section left to cover. They might just be able to stretch the last handful of salt to cover it.

Scooping up the last handful, Sam made her way around

the pool. Sweat bubbled on her forehead, but she didn't wipe it away. She let it trickle down her face, keeping her attention focused on the grains of salt resting in her palms. On the salvation they represented.

She'd made it halfway to Caroline when someone cried out.

Sam turned and saw Jenna slip. She watched as Jenna nearly lost her bead and tumbled into the water. But at the last second, the woman managed to catch herself, managed to stay on the dry deck.

However, for that split second that her attention fell away from the pool, Sam lost track of Missy. She only realized her mistake as a shriek pierced the air. As a splash echoed through the cavernous room. She spun around, but it was too late. Caroline was no longer standing on the deck. Instead, her arms thrashed in the water, the cast on her wrist weighing her down, making it nearly impossible for her to swim.

"Hang on," Sam shouted. And without thinking, she dropped the last of the salt and flung herself headfirst into the pool. She broke through the choppy surface and disappeared underneath Missy's agitated waves. She swallowed down her terror as she swam to save her best friend.

CHAPTER
TWENTY-EIGHT

Sound faded away as the water overtook Sam. She waited for fear to take hold, for panic to rise in her chest, to overwhelm her like it had at the swim meet, but this, somehow, this felt different. Her role had changed. She wasn't an unsuspecting victim anymore. She was here to save Caroline. She'd chosen to dive in. She was like her dad, coming to the rescue.

She shook out the stiffness in her arms and opened her eyes a crack. She strained to see through the water, to know where she was needed. She spotted Caroline's churning feet first, the frantic egg-beater kick barely keeping her afloat. White water crested around and underneath her. She was already tiring herself out, her cast weighing her down, keeping her from being able to make an efficient stroke. Once Missy sank her teeth in, she wouldn't last long.

Sam drifted to the bottom of the pool, then pushed off.

Even though she hadn't swum for a week, her stroke came back to her. She rocketed through the water, closing the distance fast. She reached Caroline and popped up right beside her without needing to take an extra breath.

"I'm here for you," Sam sputtered as she floated next to Caroline. "But you need to calm down. You need to save your energy. I can help pull you to the side of the pool. We can make it."

Caroline couldn't respond. She couldn't get a word out as water filled her mouth, as she barely kept her head above the surface. But she saw Sam there—realized that she wasn't alone—and it made a difference. Her arms stopped flailing and she settled down, making it possible for Sam to reach under her shoulders without getting whacked in the head.

Like that, Sam supported her best friend. She kicked and sculled and kept them both afloat. But she'd only be able to do it for so long. Sam could feel Missy in the water. She sensed her ripples and waves. She was sniffing for blood. Enjoying the hunt. She would strike soon, and Sam wouldn't be able to outswim her. Not with Caroline in tow. They'd never make it to the side of the pool. They'd never make it out.

Something nibbled at Sam's toes and she had to hold herself together. If she screamed, then Caroline would react. Sam would lose her and maybe go under, too. They couldn't swim to freedom, but maybe they could buy some time. Maybe they could trick Missy.

"I know it sounds ridiculous," Sam rattled off, hoping Caroline could hear her, that she was listening. "But play dead with me."

"What?" Caroline managed to choke out.

"You know, like dead man's float. Take a deep breath and lie facedown in the water. Let your limbs go. Let yourself drift."

"But why—"

"Just do it. Please."

Sam didn't have time to explain. She knew it was a long shot, but a lot of aquatic predators attacked by sensing movement. Maybe Missy would be the same. Maybe she'd overlook them if they played possum. If she thought they were already dead. Hadn't she let Paige go after she'd drowned?

"You ready?" Sam asked, raising a few fingers for the countdown. "Three. Two. One."

Sam sucked in the longest, deepest breath she'd ever inhaled and laid her face in the water. Going against every instinct, she let her muscles relax. She let her legs float up behind her. She let her arms go limp. She let them bob around on the surface. Her hair spread out around her, drifting on the water like seaweed. But she didn't move. She didn't breathe. She lay there and stayed absolutely still, felt Caroline doing the exact same thing next to her.

An eerie quiet settled around them. It pressed in from all sides. Sam's fingertips turned numb as a chill ran up her spine.

As the pressure in her lungs built. But Missy didn't attack. She only swirled around in the depths beneath them, moving in a figure-eight pattern, looking for but not finding them.

After about a minute, Sam's head started to throb. Her chest ached as every muscle in her body screamed for oxygen. But she couldn't take a breath. Not yet. She didn't know how they were going to get out of there, but she could prolong it. She could hope for a miracle.

A bright tang bloomed in the back of her throat, and Sam realized that her nose was bleeding. The red liquid leaked from her nostrils, turning the water in front of her eyes pink. Would Missy be able to sense that? Would she home in on her like a shark?

It hardly mattered, though, because Sam had reached her limit. If she didn't take a breath now, she'd pass out. She'd drown without Missy having to do a thing.

Sam began counting, stretching out the seconds for as long as she could. But her lungs were bursting; she couldn't hang on. Maybe she could distract Missy, though, buy Caroline some extra time to get away. Sam could put up a fight. She'd pull and kick and do everything in her power to stay afloat.

She lifted her head, prepared for the end, but as she sucked in that overdue breath, she heard a commotion coming from the shallow end. She saw Duncan up to his waist in the water, hollering and splashing like a little kid. And she saw a surge of motion responding to his diversion, making a beeline right for him.

"We have to go," Sam exclaimed as she urgently tapped Caroline on the shoulder. "Now."

The girl threw her head back, wheezing for breath, lost in an oxygen-deprived daze. But after a second, she understood. She started kicking for the wall, and Sam grabbed her and began pulling, too.

As they moved, she couldn't help worrying about Duncan. She tried to spot him in the shallow end, but there were two people splashing around now. Two people causing a distraction, dividing Missy's attention. And the second person was Bailey.

Sam couldn't believe it. But she couldn't stop and wonder about it either. She pushed on, her muscles straining, and then, finally, she reached the wall. Her hand touched solid ground and she reeled Caroline in, hoisted her up.

"We made it," Sam cried, waiting until Caroline had managed to pull herself all the way up. "We're clear."

And then, before she could talk herself out of it, she dove back in and sprinted across the pool, throwing up a huge wave of backwash, slapping the water, kicking it behind her as she made for the opposite wall, as she tried to lure Missy away so that Duncan and Bailey could escape, too.

Nearing the other side, a surge welled up behind her, a wave on the brink of cresting. Missy charged after her, snatching at her toes, a riptide ready to pull her back and sink her under. But Sam could get there. She could outswim the demon. She was faster. A champion. With a last burst of energy, she hit the wall and pulled herself out, scrambling back from the pool, making sure to step over the line of salt.

Missy's wave crashed against the deck, but they'd laid the tracks of salt thick. The water couldn't wash it away. Their barrier held and a howl pierced the air.

Sam lifted her head and was relieved to find that everyone else had made it out of the pool. Jenna had even gone around and closed their circle of protection, pinching from the thicker clumps of salt so that she had just enough to fill in the one gap. But as Missy raged in the pool, frothing and spitting and testing her boundaries, Sam realized it wouldn't hold for long. She needed to talk to her. To calm her down. To lay her spirit to rest. It was now or never.

"Missy!" Sam shouted, willing her voice to carry over the rapids, to reach the girl's ears. "I know what happened. I know how they mistreated you."

Missy let out a piercing scream as she fought against the salt barrier, as she struggled to get free.

"It wasn't right." Sam raised her voice. She remembered Caroline's lesson on intention when calling on the other side, and she injected authority into her words. She demanded an audience, insisted that Missy hear her. "You deserved better than that. You deserved a chance to keep swimming, to win more championships."

But still, Missy didn't seem to listen. The water boiled. It spat and foamed and sloshed.

"I'm sorry," Jenna cried out of nowhere. Water licked at her shoes as she stepped to the edge of the pool. As she laid herself bare for Missy. "I was young and stupid and jealous. I could never keep up. I didn't stand a chance. So, I bullied you. I won the only way I knew how."

This, finally, seemed to get Missy's attention. The water began to spiral, spinning in circles, a whirlpool forming. But then, instead of funneling down, the storm pushed up. It twisted into a tornado, a waterspout. A shape slowly emerged from the current and Missy appeared in the middle of the deep end, standing on the water, her eyes bloodred, her teeth ready to take a bite. She threw her head back and howled. She was ferocious, a demon. She was ready, at long last, to exact her revenge.

"You don't have to do this," Sam broke in, darting forward to stand on the precipice next to Jenna. "Vengeance makes us just as bad as them. As the bullies. It makes us losers."

Sam flashed back to when she'd fought Bailey in the locker room. To when Clark had nearly died. To when Paige had drowned. She hadn't felt better after any of those altercations. Vengeance hadn't solved anything. It'd only hurt other people. It'd only made her feel worse.

"We're better than that." And here, Sam paused. Her hand went to her necklace, and she pulled it off. She held it out for Missy to see, the laurel wreath dangling in front of her, the symbol that she'd once worn around her neck a reminder of what she'd wanted. What she'd strived to be. "We're champions."

Sam didn't break eye contact with Missy. She held her gaze, imploring her to listen, begging her to understand.

And suddenly, the storm began to die down. The waves quieted. Missy stood there in the middle of the pool, a stoic expression on her face, and she began to melt. Her rotted flesh dripped from her body, coming off in chunks. Her shark teeth fell out of her mouth one at a time. Her demonic exterior peeled away layer by layer until a young girl stood in front of them. Until the real Missy Caplin joined them.

She blinked, taking them all in, pausing on Jenna and Assistant Coach Carson as if she recognized them but didn't know where from. Then she glided forward, surfing on top of the water, heading right for Sam. When she reached the edge of the pool, she held out her hand, and Sam knew what she wanted. She placed the necklace in Missy's palm and nodded, okay with sacrificing Kasey's seashell, knowing it was going to a better place, knowing that she no longer needed the constant reminder because she had Caroline and Duncan now. She had her memories.

Missy closed her hand around the necklace and it disappeared, traveling along the currents of her body until it arrived at its destination, looping itself around Missy's throat, where the laurel wreath gleamed against her chest, Kasey's seashell twinkling to match.

Satisfied, Missy turned to face Jenna, she examined the girl like she would a long-lost relative, and Jenna took the opportunity to apologize again.

"I'm sorry for everything I put you through." Tears dotted Jenna's cheeks, and Sam could tell that she really was sincere. She thought that Missy could see it, too. That she could forgive.

"I miss you," Assistant Coach Carson shouted, rushing forward to get her goodbye in. The two old friends shared a long look and Sam could read all the things they were saying to each other in their wordless exchange.

After a lengthy moment, Missy retreated, moving back to the center of the pool. She smiled as she turned to face them, as a light seemed to shine from within her. And then the tension in her body gave way. A cascade of water splashed down as she came apart right in front of them. A calm washed over the pool as the water returned to its serene stillness. And Sam realized that they'd done it. That they were finally safe.

CHAPTER
TWENTY-NINE

They all stood there, frozen in the moment.

Then Duncan broke the silence. "Is it over?"

"I think so," Sam stuttered, relief slowly settling over her. She cautiously peered over the edge of the pool.

The water was placid and unbroken. There was no sign of Missy, not a single disturbance. But just to be safe, Sam took the black bead out of her pocket. The bracelet's protection hadn't been as powerful after she'd taken it apart. Or maybe Missy had just been stronger in her element. In the water. Either way, it couldn't hurt. So, Sam dropped the bead in. She watched as it sank, drifting down and down until it rested on the bottom of the pool. It nestled atop one of the black lane lines and winked up at her as it caught the light and held on to it. A pearl. A hidden treasure. She listened to the plops as everyone else followed her lead. As the black tourmaline beads came to rest in every corner of the pool.

"What were you thinking?" Duncan asked. He'd bounded around the pool, water dripping from his shaved head, just as soaked as Sam.

"What were *you* thinking?" she shot back.

"I was trying to be a hero." Duncan grimaced, but Sam could tell he didn't mean it. "And I was making sure my friend didn't drown. You should have gotten out with Caroline," he said. "You shouldn't have risked everything like that."

"Well, luckily, I'm a really good swimmer." Sam smirked as she bumped hips with him. She didn't know why she'd sprinted across the pool. In the moment, she'd just reacted. She hadn't had time to think, to worry about drowning or being afraid. But it had worked. They'd all gotten out alive. They'd all escaped.

"What I don't get," Sam began, turning to face Bailey, who, with her bathing suit on, didn't seem as out of place dripping wet, "is why you jumped in."

"You saved me," Bailey answered simply, directly. And it made perfect sense. She was the type of person who didn't want to owe anyone anything. "But don't think this makes us friends. We're even now. I'm still going to destroy you in the pool. *If* you decide to come back."

The girl sneered, and it was an expression that, unlike with Duncan, Sam knew was real. They weren't about to start liking each other, but maybe they didn't have to be foes. Maybe they could just be rivals.

"You did it!"

Sam almost fell over as Caroline collided with her, as she latched her arms around Sam's waist and drew her into a giant hug.

"Are you okay?" Sam asked as they pulled apart. "Do you feel light-headed or short of breath? You're not seeing spots or anything, are you?"

"I'm fine," Caroline replied, even though she didn't seem completely steady on her feet. "Thank you for coming in and getting me. I know it must have been terrifying. But you did it. You saved my life."

"You would have done the same for me." And it was true. They were best friends, willing to do anything for each other.

As Caroline's legs wobbled, Sam reached under her shoulder and braced her. She held her upright as Jenna and Assistant Coach Carson joined them.

"It really was her," Assistant Coach Carson marveled.

"And now you know what actually happened to her," Jenna said, guilt twisting her expression, puckering her lips. "It was an accident, but one I played a part in. If I hadn't bullied her, if I hadn't thrown her necklace into the pool that day—"

It was clear that this wasn't over for her yet. That she still had things she wanted to make right. And Sam believed that she would. The guilt still haunting her, urging her to be better, to make up for the wrongs she'd inflicted in her past.

"I'm going to make sure something like that doesn't ever

happen again," Assistant Coach Carson said. "Not here. Not on my team."

She glanced at Coach Hendricks then, at his slumped form. He was just starting to stir and an ambulance was on the way. Sam wondered how much he'd remember. If he would fight to keep his position as head coach. But he wouldn't stand a chance against Assistant Coach Carson, not when she was so determined to make a change.

"Come on," Duncan said. "Let's get out of here. I need a hot shower and some dry clothes."

Sam couldn't agree more. But as the group broke apart to head their separate ways, she paused to sneak one last glance at the pool.

"Do you think you're ready to get back in the water?" Caroline asked as she came up behind Sam. And Sam only had to think about it for a second before she answered.

"I might be."

CHAPTER
THIRTY

Sam watched the swimmers step up onto the blocks. As they crouched into their set positions, she sucked in a breath. It was a new habit. A nervousness that had cropped up in Missy's wake. She figured she'd get over it one day, but she was still learning to cope. Learning to push through it without letting it overwhelm her. When the starter beep sounded a second later, she let out a whoop, expelling that held breath and cheering on her teammates as they plunged into the water.

A lot had changed in the two weeks since they'd helped Missy's spirit find peace. Coach Hendricks had been fired, and Assistant Coach Carson had taken over control of the team.

"You ready?"

Sam turned as her dad came up behind her, a stopwatch around his neck. He had the meet's heat sheet folded under his arm and a pen stuck behind one ear.

"Don't you have a job to do?" Sam asked, lifting an eyebrow.

"I've got it covered."

Her dad clicked his stopwatch and jotted down a split as Sam's teammates made their first turn. He'd officially taken over as assistant coach the previous week. While he'd never swum himself, he'd been around the sport for Sam's whole life. He'd learned how to make up a practice. What drills they needed to do to improve their form. How to train for both endurance and sprint distances. He was a natural fit to work under Coach Carson.

"Remember what we talked about?" Sam asked.

When she'd decided to come back to swimming, she'd sat him down and had a long, honest conversation with him. She'd needed to make sure he remembered their talk. She loved the water and competing, but she couldn't handle the pressure. She wasn't going to swim personal bests every single race. She might not even win them all. But that was okay. She'd get faster in her own time. She'd enjoy the process. Enjoy being in the pool. And if that ever changed, she could walk away. She could do whatever made her happy.

"No pressure." Sam's dad held his hands up, signaling that he came in peace. "Just go out there and do your best."

Sam smiled, even though she could see that her dad wasn't completely comfortable with this new mentality. But he was working on it, making progress little by little. She knew it would take time for him to ease his competitive spirit.

"Mom will be at the next meet," she reminded him, counting down the days on her fingers. "And this time she's here to stay."

Sam practically sang this last part. This was the other big change. After months of searching, her mom had finally found a new job. She was moving up to join them in a week. They'd all be together again, something that Sam couldn't wait for. And, judging by the grin spreading across her dad's face, it was something he was excited for, too.

"I've got to get back to it," her dad said, getting serious again as he made another note on his heat sheet. "Lots of kids to coach. I can't let them think I'm favoring you."

Sam rolled her eyes and watched him go. She knew he was teasing, but she also knew that he'd have his eye on the clock the second she dove into the water. He couldn't help it.

"Good luck," Caroline cried as she skipped up behind the blocks.

A poster board flapped in her good hand. It had bright colors and number ones painted all over it, as well as peppy slogans written in glitter. Since she couldn't swim until her wrist healed, she'd taken it upon herself to be the team cheerleader. It was a good distraction. A way for her to stay involved with the team while she couldn't get in the water. And Sam had to admit that she liked having her own personal cheering section.

"Go out there and kill it," Duncan shouted as he came up

behind Caroline and looped his arm around her neck, drawing her into a little dance. They swayed back and forth, clapping their hands and stomping their feet, and Sam couldn't help but laugh. Couldn't help but feel their infectious joy.

Duncan had also changed in the past two weeks. With Clark still recovering from his run-in with Missy and Coach Carson's zero tolerance on bullying in full effect, he finally had room to breathe. To be himself. And he was thriving, even enjoying the process of letting his hair grow in as he tried out different styles.

"You're going to make me miss my race." Sam batted her friends away. She didn't want them to go, but she needed to focus because she was next up.

"We'll see you after you win," Caroline said.

"After I finish," Sam corrected them.

Again, she was trying not to put that expectation on herself. But Caroline only shrugged as Duncan dragged her away to get a good spectator spot.

By herself, Sam shed her parka and stepped up behind her block. Two lanes over, Bailey went through her prerace routine. Sam stopped and watched as the girl crouched low to the water and splashed it over her chest and arms and legs. Standing up, Bailey turned and met Sam's gaze. She held her stare.

"You better not go easy on me," she muttered, all business. "When I win, I want to know that I beat you at your best."

Sam let that sink in, adopting her own serious face as she

returned fire. "You're in luck. Because that's the only way I know how to swim."

The starter blew his whistle and Sam turned to face the pool. She stretched her goggles around her head and pressed the lenses into her eyes. She climbed onto the block, shaking her arms out, curling her toes over the edge. She tried to calm her heartbeat. She breathed in and out and in and out, focusing on the rhythm, on keeping it steady. She checked her goggle straps again. She tucked her chin into her chest. She grabbed the block, coiled her muscles, and waited.

When the starter's beep sounded, Sam didn't hesitate. She threw herself forward, soaring and then plummeting, breaking through the surface of the water. Its cool waves washed over her as she kicked and glided and cut through the current. When she popped up and took her first stroke, her worries slipped away and she swam, unafraid of what might be hiding in the depths. Confident that she could face it.